MW00944413

The Education of Charlotte Royce

an Erotic Regency Romance Novel

Loreli Love

To all who love well-crafted erotic tales that favor
titillating delights, love and happy endings

CONTENTS

1 CHARLOTTE ARRIVES AT WHARTON MANSE

Charlotte Royce first glimpsed the looming towers of Wharton Manse through the twilight mist as the carriage rolled up the long gravel drive . She felt a shiver of apprehension and shrank back against the velvet cushions of the carriage, ensconcing herself more deeply in the black wool traveling cloak.

She had only just left Quigley Hall this morning shortly before sunrise and already she felt homesick. She had never traveled any further than Lawton, the village three miles from her family home, and she felt little prepared to deal with the enormity of the dark foreboding towers awaiting her.

Her father's untimely death had left her mother, herself and her two younger sisters in unfortunate financial straits. It was only from necessity and her concern for her family's well-being that she had agreed to marry Sir Edmund Prescott, Earl of Wharton.

She shuddered to remember the fateful day of her engagement. Her beloved father had only been laid to rest for three hours before Sir Prescott approached her and let her know in no uncertain terms what her family's fate would be if she did not comply with his request.

He had cornered her in the parlor when the rest of the funeral party was still in the drawing room eating the late afternoon repast. He was almost three times her age with a full head of gray hair, but he held his tall and trim physique ramrod straight. He towered over her that afternoon of her father's funeral when he approached her and took her black-gloved hand in his.

"Your home is entailed, my dear, and as you are aware, your poor father left you no income," he said. Though pushing sixty, his voice was yet deep and resonant, and his hand firmly held hers when she sought to pull away. "Only you have the power to keep your family safe from destitution."

He had looked down into her blue eyes, his black eyes dark and intense under the graying brows. He pulled her closer to him, grasping both her hands in his.

Living as she had in the seclusion of Quigley Hall, she had not had much experience with the manly sex. She did not know how to read the deepening darkness of his eyes or the flush creeping up his neck above the cravat. His breath had quickened and when he suddenly jerked her against him, his hands now holding hers behind her and forcing her body against his, she couldn't help the involuntary rush of air into her lungs that pushed her breasts against his chest. She did not know what it was that pushed hard against her stomach, though she thought it might be a belt buckle.

His breath came unevenly when he spoke next. "If you were to marry me, the Prescott fortune would be at your command. My family's money and power would enable you to retain Quigley Hall and your mother and delightful little sisters would not have to lose their home."

Charlotte tried to focus on what he was saying but she had never been held so close by a man. The physical contact was distracting, and she felt assaulted not just by the hard lines of his body that thrust against her but also by the alien, pungent scent he exuded. Without thinking, she drew in a breath to clear her mind, but it forced her corseted breasts more firmly against him, and she was unprepared for his reaction.

"To hell with convention," he cursed. His head swooped down and she found herself being kissed for the first time.

It was nothing like what she had fantasized about or read in the few scandal novels she had managed to obtain. He was not the debonair Prince Charming, young and virile, and the kiss was not an earth-shattering moment. Instead, she felt his thin lips hard on hers. She did not know to open her mouth to the tongue that fleetingly touched her lips.

She did know that what he said was true about her family's desperate financial situation and that she would have to accept his offer of marriage in order to save her family. No other suitors had visited Quigley Hall, because her father had thought that at her tender age, she was still too young for the marriage mart. Sir Prescott had done business with her father, which had brought him in contact with her. The only other suitable man she had ever met was Reverend Markham, who presided over the Lawton Parish. She had often daydreamed about the attractive minister, but he had only the meager stipend of a country pastor and would not be able to save Quigley Hall from the Prattles, her cousins to whom the estate was entailed.

She twisted her head aside from the probing lips and gasped, "You are right, Sir. I will marry you."

With her words, he relaxed his grip on her, though he retained his hold on her hands and drew her to the settee and sat her down. Standing over her, his hands still firmly holding hers, a smooth smile touched his lips. "You have made me the happiest of men."

The rest of the day had passed in a blur for Charlotte, the funeral party suddenly transforming itself into an engagement party. Though she had felt relieved for the future of her family, she could not feel happy for herself and dreaded the thought of her own future when she would have to leave her home and become the Lady Prescott.

Sir Prescott was a man who abided by tradition, and as such, believed in observing mourning etiquette. He permitted Charlotte to stay with her family at Quigley Hall for the one-year mourning period. Unspoken, but undoubtedly part of his plan, was for her to come of age. Society might still look askance at his marrying such a young girl, but at least she could not be considered a child. She had gratefully accepted the delay of her impending future and was thankful that Sir Prescott's business kept his visits to Quigley Hall considerably infrequent. In the year since his proposal, she had only seen him twice in the presence of her mother and sisters.

But now, she was alone and about to set foot in his domain for the first time. In the letter he sent requesting (though truly it had been a demand) that the engagement move forward, he had assured her mother that there would be several other guests at Wharton House including his cousin Barbara, who would act as chaperone for her daughter. Charlotte wished her mother could have accompanied her but that would have meant doing the unthinkable and leaving her sisters alone at Quigley Hall. Neither she nor her mother had felt in the position to request that Sir Prescott entertain their entire family at his country estate. Perhaps when they were married, but not yet. So, she had come alone.

The carriage came to a stop in front of the three story stone edifice that was Wharton Manse. The front door opened and a portly man with a full black beard and dressed in formal butler attire descended the steps. He pulled open the carriage door and handed her down, his brown eyes traveling over her boldly as he spoke.

"Welcome to Wharton Manse, Miss. I be Hornby, the butler."

Something about how he looked at her made her feel self-conscious. She wanted to pull her gloved hand from his, where he pressed it against his protuberant stomach, but she didn't want to appear rude. He ushered her up the stairs and into the building. A young woman in a black and white maid's outfit stood directly inside.

"The Master wanted to greet ye himself, but he was called away this morn on business. With luck, he will be home in time for dinner. In the meanwhile, Alice here will show ye to yer rooms."

"Nice to meet you, Miss," Alice said, curtsying, and then led the way up an imposing marble staircase. Hornby followed with her traveling case.

The room to which she was shown caused her to stifle a gasp of astonishment. It was enormous, at least twice the size of her old room at Quigley Hall. Just the bed alone with its crimson velvet drapes and massive mahogany headboard could have filled her room back home.

"Ye be needing some hot water, I'm sure, to freshen up after yer long journey before dinner, Miss," Alice said and left the room.

Charlotte took a deep breath, thankful for the moment alone, and walked to the large window. The window opened onto a second floor balcony and she could see the sun finally peep out beneath the thick clouds that had kept the day dark and cold. She pushed open the window and stepped out onto the balcony, wanting to feel the faint rays of the setting sun on her face.

Below her, she could see a formal garden and beyond that an open field. Further off, a dense forest bordered the horizon. The oncoming evening would be cold and she smelled rain in the breeze that chilled her skin. She turned her face to the sun and enjoyed the last moments before sunset.

Suddenly, she felt self-conscious, as though eyes were watching her. Looking down across the formal garden into the gathering gloom, she caught the flash of something or someone moving between the bushes. A chill unrelated to the night crept through her and she hastily retreated back into the safety of her room.

"Ye be likin' the view?" Alice had returned with the steaming bowl of water.

"Quite," Charlotte said and dismissed the maid.

**

After washing up, Charlotte stood in her petticoat and considered her wardrobe. She looked at the three dresses hanging in the armoire. Even her petticoat had been mended several times, and the three dresses were growing threadbare. There was her pink gingham, but that was a day dress, which wouldn't be appropriate for a formal dinner, and then there was her gray wool, which she had traveled in and had worn the day of her father's funeral. The last dress was a dark blue that set off her blue eyes and long blond hair to advantage.

She shrugged into it and studied herself in the full-length mirror that stood across from her bed. Her long blond hair hung in two braids down her back. Her mother had just shown her several days earlier how to pin it up in a crown on her head, which was how she had worn it for the trip, hoping it made her look more like a woman of age.

She gathered the pins and winced as she put her hair up again, her scalp tender from the weight pulling on it. The dress was made of silk with a high waistband. Recently, her bust line had grown and her mother had had to make adjustments to the dress. She straightened the white kerchief that her mother had designed to fit in place above her bosom to hide the cleavage she had developed. Though she suspected the dress was hopelessly out of style, there was nothing she could do, and such as it was, she did think the dress set off her figure to advantage.

Straightening her shoulders and summoning her courage, she pushed open the door to her room and headed down the hall.

Her slippers made no sound as she padded along the runway carpet of the hallway. As she passed one of the rooms, she heard a strange noise. It sounded almost like an animal in pain. Stopping, she looked through the door that stood partly ajar.

At first, she couldn't discern what she was seeing, but then she realized a man was standing between a woman's legs. All she could see was from her vantage point was the back of the man as he stood, his pants about his thighs, and his bare bottom moving back and forth. He seemed tall, his dark hair tied in a cue at the back of his neck, and he was in his shirtsleeves. The woman's white legs were plump and bare except for red mules and were wrapped around his waist. Charlotte heard the sound again and realized it was the man grunting as he moved back and forth. Her surprised breath caught in her throat and she hurried on, afraid to be caught witnessing such unseemly behavior. She had never thought about what men and women did in private, much less seen such a thing. The image was unsettling and disturbing.

"Ye be lost, Miss?"

Hornby the butler suddenly appeared beside her, and she involuntarily shuddered when she saw how his lips glistened red and wet behind his beard. His brown eyes seemed to bore into hers. She had never had experience with a butler before. At Quigley Hall, they had only been able to afford two servants. She had grown up with Alfred and Nellie, who had been like family to her. This Hornby fellow seemed too familiar for a butler, but she wasn't sure exactly how butlers were supposed to behave.

"I was looking for the dining room," she said, avoiding his probing eyes and moving away from him.

"Ye be headed the wrong way, Miss," he said and took her arm.

She hurriedly pulled away from him. "I don't want to be any bother and I'm sure I can find it on my own, if you just point me the right way."

"Oh Miss, ye definitely point me in the right way," Hornby snickered, staring boorishly at her bosom.

"You must be Miss Charlotte," a female voice suddenly interrupted.

Charlotte looked thankfully at the woman who had just approached where she and Hornby stood in the hallway.

"I'm Barbara Geary, Edmund's cousin." The woman extended a gloved hand to Charlotte.

She shook Barbara's hand but tried to keep from staring at her. Charlotte guessed the woman was in her late thirties, or maybe early forties, with a glorious head of dark red hair and dressed in the most provocative and yet beautiful dress she had ever seen. It was a rich green sateen with a full skirt and plunging neckline. Charlotte had to tear her eyes from the woman's bosom, which looked like it might at any moment spring free from where it was barely confined by the dress.

"Pleased to meet you, ma'am," Charlotte said.

Barbara broke into a throaty laugh. "Please, call me Barbara, or at least Cousin. I may be almost old enough to be your mother, but you don't have to remind me."

"Oh, I'm sorry, ma'am -- I mean Barbara," Charlotte said, flustered. She was further flustered when she dropped her eyes in embarrassment and realized Barbara was wearing red mules. This was the woman she had just seen in a dalliance with a man! Charlotte blushed.

"Oh, my dear, it's nothing to be embarrassed about," Barbara broke into her thoughts, mistaking her beet red face.

Charlotte's eyes flew upwards from the red shoes, past the most cleavage she had ever seen, to the woman's sherry-colored eyes. "Of course," she cleared her throat, hoping she sounded collected.

"Come, let us go to dine." Barbara took her arm. "I

sure hope Edmund knows what he's doing," she laughed under her breath as they breezed by Hornby, who stood staring while they passed. Charlotte saw his tongue flick out and lick his fat red lips before she hurriedly looked away.

They walked past several more stately rooms and down the sweeping marble staircase, past tapestries and gold-framed paintings into a massive dining room with twinkling chandeliers, a baronial fireplace, and a table set for six. Several servants pulled back chairs as they entered the room.

"I see we are the first here," Barbara said. "Would you like some wine?"

Charlotte had only once had spirits before, on the occasion of her father's funeral, but she did not want to appear young and naive.

"Please," she nodded to the servant who stood behind her chair. He gracefully filled her crystal goblet with a clear red liquid.

Just then, another woman entered the room.

"Sally, good. Come sit by me." Barbara patted the seat next to her. Charlotte sat directly across from them.

"This is Charlotte Royce, Edmund's betrothed."

"How very nice to meet you." Sally looked over Charlotte briefly and then tittered. "I thought he liked them a little more worldly, didn't he?" she said sotto voce to Barbara.

Charlotte did not understand precisely what Sally meant, though she suspected the woman was referring to Edmund's preference in women. It seemed rude to talk about her as though she were not in the room, but she was unsure what constituted proper etiquette for Society.

Though not as daring as Barbara's plunging neckline, Sally's dress revealed her feminine attributes it its own way. The bodice was created with some kind of thin material, so fine that even across the table Charlotte could swear she saw the darkening of Sally's nipples through the pale cream fabric. Unlike the tight material of Barbara's dress, Sally's was loose, and when she moved, Charlotte could see her breasts sway through the thin fabric.

She forced her eyes back to Sally's face. She guessed Sally to be at least ten years younger than Barbara, and unlike the older woman, she wore no wedding ring. Her hair was a light brown and worn in short curls about her head.

Before Barbara could respond to Sally's comment, two men entered the room. The first was an older gentleman, shorter than the second, with a balding pate and a large belly squeezed into his burgundy dinner jacket. The second man was not many years older than she, tall and slim, with dark hair tied back in a queue. Charlotte stifled a gasp and looked down at her glass of wine, hoping to hide her face, which she felt flame in embarrassment. She was certain this was the man she had seen dallying with Barbara.

Unfortunately, he approached and stood beside her at the table, so she was forced to look up.

Barbara made the introductions. "William, this is Miss Charlotte Royce, Edmund's intended. Charlotte, this is William Hathaway, and this is William, my husband," she gestured to the older man who squeezed into the chair at one end of the table.

"How do you do?" Charlotte said, only belatedly realizing the young man standing next to her was waiting to kiss her hand as part of the introduction.

She felt another blush begin when she realized her faux pas, and then, when he took her bare hand in his and pressed his smooth lips to the back of it, she looked up startled at the sensation. No man had ever kissed her bare hand before and her eyes flew to his, shocked to find herself staring into the face of the most handsome man she had ever seen. His eyes were a light gray, striking under the black brows, his chin strong, his lips sensuously shaped.

She felt her face flame red and the man chuckled, briefly squeezing her hand.

"I'm doing just fine," he said. His voice was deep and resonant.

She tore her eyes from him, chastising her errant thoughts and wishing she had the worldly demeanor of the women sitting across from her. She fought to focus on the conversation that was transpiring between Barbara and her husband, but she couldn't stop the shiver of awareness as William sat beside her. She could feel the warmth emanating from his body, and she couldn't help starting violently when he pulled his chair closer to the table and his thigh came in contact with her leg. She hastily pulled away, but to her shock, he pushed his leg over and against her thigh once more.

She could only assume from his behavior and after what she had seen in the room upstairs that William was a rake. She had read about them in those scandal novels and how they were always in pursuit of women. She wouldn't give him the satisfaction of letting him know he had flustered her, so she refused to look at him, though she felt the beginnings of a blush creep up her neck. She tried to squelch it. Unfortunately, she was trapped by at the end corner of the table, so she was unable to pull her leg out of contact with his. When she felt his leg slowly move against hers, she hastily took another sip of wine, wishing etiquette would allow her to take her hands off the table so she could push him away.

"Edmund should be here in time for the meat," Sir Geary was saying as he helped himself to a serving of soup. "I'm sure you are looking forward to seeing your betrothed."

Charlotte nodded and realized she felt a little lightheaded. It must be the wine, she thought.

The conversation steered toward a hunting party and a ball planned for the following week. Charlotte felt completely out of her element, having never ridden a horse or attended a ball. She listened and observed the dynamics and tried to ignore William, who continued to rub his leg periodically against hers under the table. He also sought every opportunity to fill her wineglass and she realized rather belatedly that he was getting her drunk. She lost track of the conversation again, though she got the sense that Barbara was flirting rather obviously with William, leaning across the table to expose her cleavage to him when she laughed at his jokes. Her husband seemed oblivious to anything but food and wine, eating and drinking at a remarkable rate. Sally seemed a voyeur, watching and laughing knowingly at all the goings on.

Hornby appeared at the door and announced, "The Master has arrived."

Within moments, Charlotte found herself standing, the servant having removed her chair. She swayed, feeling the full effects of the wine.

"Easy there," William said in a low voice, his hand closing over her bare upper arm to steady her. In the instant before he released her, she thought she felt his fingers caress the tender inner side of her arm and she inhaled, surprised.

But then Edmund was there, tall and distinguished, standing before her, kissing her bare hand and looking into her eyes. She looked up into his black eyes and timidly smiled.

"My dear, I hope you have been made to feel welcome in my home," he said.

Charlotte nodded, hating herself for it, but unable to stop the blush spreading up her throat as she remembered what she had seen upstairs and William behavior toward her this evening.

Edmund didn't seem to notice her embarrassment and turned to his friends. "Welcome everyone. I am sorry I was delayed, but I am glad to have not missed this wonderful repast."

He took the seat at the end of the table, so now

Charlotte was hemmed in on one side by William and by her fiancé on the other. Fortunately, Edmund kept his legs to himself, but to her surprise, William did not view her fiancé's being there as reason to stop rubbing his leg against hers.

The dinner conversation flowed around her and Charlotte tried to make sure she nodded when she was supposed to. Other than that, she felt completely out of her league, the conversation ranging from international affairs to London Society gossip, none of which she knew anything about.

Eventually, she noticed everyone else rise to their feet, so she followed their lead.

"We'll leave the men to their port," Barbara announced. "Let us ladies retire to the parlor."

Charlotte managed not to stumble, though she still felt lightheaded as she followed Barbara and Sally through another door and into a smaller, cozier room. A warm fire glowed in the grate.

"Would you like a sherry, my dear?" Barbara asked.

Charlotte collapsed onto one of the settees, forgetting to maintain her posture. "No thanks, ma'am," she said.

Sally laughed at Barbara's frown. "Don't go too hard on the girl, Bonnie, I do believe she's in her cups."

"Charlotte, I told you to please address me as 'Barbara,' or 'Bonnie,' or even Cousin." Barbara ignored Sally and moved to stand before Charlotte.

Charlotte forced herself straight on the settee. "I'm sorry, Cousin, I'm feeling a little tired."

Barbara looked down at her and laughed. "You are looking a little rough around the edges."

While Charlotte lightly dosed on the settee, she could hear the other two women speaking softly to each other.

"I really have no idea what on earth Edmund was thinking," Barbara said.

"Her family is genteel, but of no consequence," Sally murmured in agreement. "It really makes no sense. You know both Annie and Hettie are nothing like her, not in terms of age or features."

"I'm not so sure. That hideous rag she is wearing hides her attributes. And she certainly is youthful."

At that, Sally laughed. "He must feel the need to produce an heir, and who better than some young thing like her? That is the only explanation I can think of that makes any sense."

Charlotte found herself drowsily wondering the same thing. It was obvious why she had accepted Edmund's proposal, but why had he bothered to propose to her? She may be provincial and naive, but she was certain that a man of his stature could have any woman he desired. He was extremely wealthy, and though he was older, he was still attractive in a distinguished sort of way. She vaguely wondered who Annie and Hettie were, but then forgot about them as the men entered the room and she found Edmund at her side. He settled himself beside her on the settee, and she found herself practically in his arms. She leaned against his shoulder and was surprised to find it comforting. He took her hands in his and feathered a kiss across her knuckles.

"My poor dear, you look out on your feet," he whispered. "I think it is time you went to bed."

He stood and brought her up with him. She swayed against him and he laughed.

"I will be back down to join you all shortly after I see my intended to her room."

The next thing Charlotte knew, Edmund was standing close beside her outside her bedroom door, his arms around her, supporting her and pressing her against his firm body.

"I have missed you, my sweet," he said and bent to press a kiss on her lips.

Woozily, she realized the sensation was pleasant, and she smiled against his mouth.

He pulled back and looked down into her blue eyes. "I

do believe you enjoyed that," he said, bringing his hands to her hips and gently coaxing her closer to him.

Again she felt his belt buckle press stiffly against her stomach as it had the day of her father's funeral when he had kissed her.

"We will need to do something about your wardrobe," he said, looking down at her dress.

Then, to her surprise, she felt him pull the kerchief away from her bosom. Belatedly, she realized she should have stopped him. She was unprepared for his reaction, his sharp intake of breath and the narrowed intensity of his gaze. A red flush crept up his neck and the hardness pressing against her stomach seemed strangely to grow bigger.

"My little girl is growing up," he muttered, and before she realized what he was about to do, his hand came up and traced the large mounds of her breasts that were now exposed above the low bodice and tight corset of her dress.

She gasped at the sensation and was startled to feel her nipples harden against the corset's restraint.

"You are much too beautiful to remain hidden," he groaned and his hand swept once more across her breasts. Then, to her absolute shock, he bent his head and placed a kiss on the full, delicate mound of her left breast. He put his hands on her hips once more and moved slightly back, a look of what she thought looked like disappointment on his face.

"I would help you undress for bed, my dear, but I don't think even I have the discipline to keep it to that," he sighed and backed away from her, pressing one last lingering kiss on the palm of her hand. "I will call Alice to help you prepare for bed."

*****

2 CHARLOTTE'S EDUCATION BEGINS

The next morning, Charlotte awoke with a headache. She looked out the window at the gray and rainy day and thought that perhaps it was the residual effects of the wine that made her forehead pound. A knock sounded on her door.

"Come in," she said.

"Breakfast is now being served in the breakfast room, Miss," Alice said. "You be wanting me to help you dress?"

Charlotte pulled her frayed wrapper more tightly around her nightgown. "Thank-you, but no. I have a bit of a headache. Would you be so kind as to send up a little tea?" She sat down on the chair in front of the vanity table, her blond hair hanging long and unbound down her back.

"But certainly, Miss." Alice disappeared.

As soon as the maid had gone, Charlotte returned to bed. Not more than ten minutes later, the door opened again.

"My lord?" Charlotte blushed in dismay to find Sir Prescott entering the room, a tea tray balanced precariously in one of his arms. She made to rise from the bed.

"No need to rise, my dear. I thought I would do you the honors of bringing you breakfast in bed. Alice tells me you are not feeling well."

"It is nothing, just a slight headache. I'm sure it will be gone soon."

"Nonsense, my dear. We can't have you spending your first full day at Wharton Manse not up to snuff." He set the tray across her thighs where she lay in the bed, effectively trapping her.

She wiggled to sit up, and to her surprise, Sir Prescott came close with a pillow.

"Please, allow me." His breath was warm in her ear as he pushed the pillow behind her back. She could smell the distinctive, expensive scent of his cologne, mixed with something darker, a more male scent. Her eyes flew to his, wanting to know what he was thinking.

He looked as old as her father, but he had aged much more gracefully. Where her father had gained a great deal of weight in his last years, Sir Prescott was tall and trim and looked to be in excellent physical shape. She stared at him, realizing that except for his age, he in no way resembled her father. For all his years, Sir Prescott was a distinguished-looking older gentleman. She was disturbed to find herself enjoying his attentions and his manly presence in her room, though she was unsure of the proper behavior. He looked kindly down at her, taking her hands in his and pressing feather kisses on the back of both her hands.

"Good morning, my sweet," he said. "Let me pour you your tea." He sat down on the bed, his thigh pressing gently against her soft hip.

She remembered the night before and William' leg rubbing against hers at the dinner table. She fought the blush that slowly heated her face.

"Here you are." He handed her the cup, just in time to take in her flushed features. He smiled then, in his slightly patronizing way. "I forget that you are yet unfamiliar with the domestic bliss of married folk."

She found herself blushing more deeply as his gaze wandered over her face and down to her breasts. She had taken off the wrapper when she returned to bed. Now she wished she had it about her and could pull it tight over her threadbare nightgown. Remembering Sally's provocative see-through dress, Charlotte suspected Sir Prescott could see just as much now.

His black eyes seemed to darken further as he gazed upon her and one of his hands came up to smooth the bed sheets over her hips. She stifled a gasp when she felt his hand caress her thigh. Even through the thick covers, his hand felt bony yet strong.

"There are many advantages to marriage, as I have determined. With my greater age and experience, it is only reasonable that I shall need to tutor you in the proper way a wife may please her husband. And of course, how I may please you."

He slowly pulled down the covers. Charlotte had her hands full, one with a teacup, the other with a piece of toast. She watched helplessly as the covers slipped to her waist, and then to her legs.

"That's better." His voice had deepened and he stared intently at her body.

She put the toast back on the plate, her mouth dry, and took another sip of tea before putting the cup down with a clatter.

Abruptly, he stood. "Let me remove this, now that you have finished your meal."

He lifted the tray off her and set it on the bedside table. She hastily pulled the covers back up to her chin, hoping he might now leave the room.

"How is your head feeling?" He sat down again, this time even closer to her on the bed, his thigh pressing firmly into her waist.

"Fine, I'm feeling fine, thank-you," she answered quickly, hoping he would stop the solicitous behavior. She worried what he would do next.

"No headache?" He reached out a hand and smoothed it across her brow.

She couldn't bite back the gasp of surprise at the intimacy of the gesture. "No, it has gone," she whispered, realizing that indeed with his presence in the room, she had forgotten all about her headache. She was having trouble thinking about anything else.

"You still seem very tense. Give me your hands," he commanded, his voice deep.

Her eyes flew to his, unsure what he would do if she refused. She nibbled her full bottom lip and considered him for a moment.

"My dear, I mean you no harm. I will never hurt you. You must understand that I only have your best intentions in mind. Now, please, give me your hands. You will feel much better, I promise you." His eyes were dark and intense, almost hypnotic under the graying brows.

She found herself thinking abstractly that he had aged very agreeably, his jaw line still firm, the lines on his face revealing that smiles visited his face more often than frowns. A slight smile touched his thin lips now, quirking one side up slightly.

She pulled her arms out from under the covers and held them out. She began to feel overly warm.

"Very good, my dear. You are learning."

He took her hands in his and slid even closer to her on the bed. She could smell his scent again, his hands hard on hers. Then, he brought both her hands to his lips. She watched in astounded fascination as he gently slid her right index finger into his mouth.

She gasped. The sensation was unlike anything she had ever felt before and the image of her young finger disappearing between his firm, thin lips was surprisingly erotic. Slowly, one by one, he kissed and nibbled on all of her fingers, muttering words of encouragement as he went along.

"That's good, there you go, now you're learning how to please me." At moments, he would look up and study her face, taking in the flushed, heated coloring. She was now much too overheated for the bedcovers, which were still pulled up under her chin.

"You look a little warm, my dear. Let me help you," he whispered, his voice deepening as he bent over her, using both hands to slowly pull the coverlet down. "There, isn't that better?" he asked, resuming his attentions to her fingers, though she noticed his eyes kept straying down her body. He had pulled the covers below her waist.

She shifted on the bed, aware of a dampening wetness between her legs. She wondered if she were sweating.

He watched her movements and she heard his breath hitch and begin to change tempo.

"You look like you are still uncomfortable. Here, let me cool you sufficiently," he said, his voice husky.

He still held both her hands in one of his. With the other, he reached out and pulled on the ribbon at the neck of her nightgown. For a moment, she tried to retrieve her hands to stop him. He held them firm against his lap.

"Don't worry, my sweet," he murmured. "I am only trying to help."

And then he pushed her nightgown aside, revealing her full white breasts. She blushed deeply to feel him staring at her.

"You are even more beautiful than I imagined," he breathed.

After what seemed like endless moments with him staring and her heart racing in embarrassment and perhaps something else, with his free hand, he reached out and touched her breasts.

"No, please!" she gasped, alarmed at the wildfire coursing through her veins when she felt his cool hand on her fevered flesh.

"One lesson you will need to learn, my dear, is that you must never deny me." His fingers closed around her distended nipple and squeezed. The sensation was pure torture, almost pain, but also something else. The moisture wet her nightgown further and she stifled the urge to squirm her legs together.

"Do you understand me?" Sir Prescott said, his thumb and forefinger mercilessly teasing first one and then the other nipple.

Charlotte bit back a moan as she felt her nipples erect to diamond hard points. She couldn't help squirming then, her legs sliding against each other as she sought relief from the wild sensations coursing through her body. He was driving her mad. Maybe if she agreed with him, he would stop the sensual torment.

"Yes, I understand," she panted.

"Good, now I am going to release your hands and I want you to put them at your sides."

Charlotte nodded, unable to speak when both his hands closed over her breasts and began molding and kneading them. She couldn't believe how sensitive they had become and they seemed to swell larger under his ministrations.

Just when she thought she was being driven to distraction with how he was touching her, endlessly squeezing and kneading her breasts, his thumbs brushing her nipples to aching sensitivity, he dipped his head and fastened his mouth around her breast.

"Oh heavens!" she cried out, unable to stop her body from writhing sinuously on the bed.

Over and over he suckled first one breast while teasing the other with his hand, and then he would switch position. She thought she would die from the intensity of sensation. Her body was on fire.

"Please, please," she moaned, not sure what she was asking of him as she watched his gray head move between her breasts.

Then, when she thought she would explode, he sat back on the bed, taking her hands in his again and studying her expression, his eyes dipping to observe her naked breasts that tingled and burned with sensation.

"Beautiful, my dear. You are beautiful when you look at me with such heat, such passion. You are a good student."

For a moment, she noticed one of his hands straying to his breeches while he studied her. He seemed to adjust something. Her eyes flew back to his and she noticed the red flush darkening his face. He licked his lips and drew a deep, steadying breath.

"I think that is enough for your first lesson."

He stood and she immediately pulled the bed covers up.

"Not yet, my dear. Please wait until I have left. I want to remember you like this."

He bent over her and swept the covers from her, again revealing her aching breasts. They instantly erected with the friction of the covers sliding over their sensitized flesh and the cool air of the room.

"So beautiful," he murmured and leaned over her, suckling each breast one last time.

She could not stop the gasp of pleasure, for now she realized she enjoyed the feel of his mouth on her. As he left his final moist kiss, his groin brushed against her hand where it lay on the comforter. She felt something stiff protruding from his breeches.

When he stood beside the bed, his groin came to eye-level with where she sat on the bed. Her eyes flew to the front of his breeches. What was that huge protuberance? For a startled moment, Charlotte wondered if he were deformed in some way. On other occasions, she had felt it and thought it a belt buckle, but now, she realized he must have some kind of physical deformity. She forced her eyes from it to his face and blushed when she realized he was watching her. Heavens, she hoped he didn't think her rude, staring at what was obviously something unusual about him.

He smiled, taking her hand in his. "You little minx, you like what you see."

To her dismay, he placed her hand against the protuberance. It was long, very hard and surprisingly warm to the touch. Charlotte tried to pull away, but he tightened his hold on her.

"Oh, that's good," he groaned and rubbed her hand against it. Then, he bit back an oath and brought her hand to his lips. "We must stop, my sweet. Your passionate nature has led me to take you further with your lessons than is appropriate for now. But don't worry," he said, sucking one last time on her tingling finger and watching her intently.

She was unable to keep from curling her toes, her bare breasts again erecting, and her body moving sensuously over the bed when his tongue teased the space between her thumb and forefinger.

He smiled when he saw her response. "You are learning well." He sounded pleased and then picked up the tea tray. "Now that you are feeling better, I hope you are ready for a visit from the modiste. Barbara is determined that we have you dressed appropriately to your station as my intended, and I suppose she is right. Sally and she are expecting you in the second floor parlor within the hour." With those words and a slow lingering glance at her breasts, Sir Prescott left the room.

Charlotte collapsed on the bed as soon as the door closed, unable to believe what had just transpired. Her fingers tingled, her nipples ached, her body felt awash in a sea of sensation she had never before experienced.

She touched her fingers to her lips. Did other fiancés do that to their betrothed's fingers? Her hands slid to her breasts. So large, they overflowed her hands, she touched them and sighed in pleasure. Never had she thought that they would feel like this, and when she touched her nipples that stabbed diamond hard into her palms, she moaned with sensation.

She threw back the covers and stepped from the bed, her nightgown slipping from her. Naked and standing in front of the full-length mirror, she looked critically at her body, wanting to see what Sir Prescott had seen.

She almost didn't recognize herself. Her long blond hair lay disheveled about her face and the color in her cheeks glowed unnaturally red. Her eyes sparkled a deep blue. She looked lower, she noticed a pink hue darkening her neck and the tops of her breasts. Gazing at her breasts, she was astonished yet again to see how much they had grown in the last few months, at least double in size from before, and her nipples were puckered as if she were cold, and brightly pink. She ran a hand down her stomach to the juncture between her legs. She was surprised to find the wetness dampening her blond curls there.

A knock on the door jerked her out of her reverie and she grabbed the nightgown from the floor and clamped it quickly to her.

Alice peeked in. "You be needing me to dress you, miss?"

Charlotte thought of her appointment with the two older women. It would probably be best if she were fully corseted for her appointment with the modiste. "Please, Alice."

She removed the nightgown, and Alice paused, holding the corset in her hands as she stared in the mirror at Charlotte's naked image.

"You be a beautiful young woman." Alice was a good head taller than Charlotte and bony thin. Charlotte guessed she was probably five years older than herself.

"Thank-you Alice." Charlotte smiled shyly and hastily pulled the corset around her slim waist, tucking her generous breasts into the corset's confines.

"Me thinks Sir Prescott made a good choice, if you don't mind my saying, Miss. Them poor dresses you have hide your beauty. You should dress like Lady Barbara and Miss Sally, you should," Alice nodded as she cinched the laces firmly about Charlotte's waist, causing Charlotte's breasts to rise upwards into large pale mounds above their restraints.

Charlotte shivered in sensual awareness, surprised that she enjoyed the feeling of the material rasping against her tender, sensitized flesh.

"I'll wear the pink gingham." Charlotte pointed to the threadbare daydress hanging in the armoire.

Alice helped her into it. As with the blue dress she had worn the previous night, her mother had adjusted this one to accommodate her expanding bust size. When she picked up the white kerchief to tuck it into the bodice, Alice clucked.

"Oh no, Miss. If I may be so bold, you should leave be with the kerchief. The dress is nothing to look at, but your attributes, they are most pleasing."

Charlotte looked in the mirror, seeing how the dress barely covered her nipples, which seemed to have stayed permanently erect following Sir Prescott's meticulous attentions. They pressed against the corset and the loose material of the bodice and she could see how large and pale her breasts appeared as they bulged above the low neckline. Again she found herself staring at her bosom, surprised at the sight. The woman standing before her in the mirror seemed a voluptuously endowed adult, not the young, naively innocent girl she felt herself to be.

Alice quickly braided her hair into a long plait down her back and then looked at the clock on the mantle. "It be time to go, Miss. Lady Barbara don't like to be kept waiting."

"Of course."

Charlotte followed Alice into the hall, surprised to feel moisture still wetting the blond curls at the juncture of her thighs.

"If you please, Miss, go down that hall and turn left. The second floor parlor is the final room on the right." Alice directed Charlotte to her appointment with the modiste.

Wharton Manse was the grandest place Charlotte had ever seen and she walked slowly, admiring the paintings and gigantic tapestries that lined the walls on each side of the magnificent hallway. She reached the end of the main hall and took a left, as per Alice's instructions. As she turned the corner, Hornby the portly butler approached from the adjoining hall.

"Ah, Miss Charlotte." His eyes never even met hers. Instead, they focused completely on her cleavage. His beefy hand came up to wipe his beard and his tongue wiped across his red lips. "If ye will please come this way. I have something I need with ye."

"I don't have time at the moment, Hornby. I am wanted in the second floor parlor immediately."

He made her nervous with his strangely intense gaze and his odd behavior. She tried to move past him, but to her bewilderment, he seized her arm and rushed her into the small room beside where they stood. He closed the door behind him and leaned against it, his breathing labored and an unnatural red tingeing his flesh above his bushy black beard. His black eyes glinted.

"What on earth is the matter with you?" Charlotte demanded, her voice rising as she realized with fright that he had trapped her in the room. She looked about for another escape route, but besides the one window, there was none other than the door he was leaning against.

"Nothing that a few moments with ye won't cure, Miss," he grunted.

She stared in alarm as his hand moved lower, beneath his belly that was barely concealed in the butler's uniform, to the buttons of his black breeches. Shocked, she saw that he, like Sir Prescott, seemed to have a deformity there, but then he finished unbuttoning his pants.

She tried to still the unruly beating of her heart and took several deep breaths to try and calm her fear, but the action caused her breasts to surge upwards, their mounds swelling over the bodice of her dress. The butler leered, never taking his eyes from her heaving breasts. She was sure he could see her nipples, which had remained erect and kept her in a constant state of torment and sensual awareness.

Hornby licked his lips as he pulled what looked like some kind of red baton from his breeches. Charlotte couldn't help but stare as he gripped the piece of flesh in his fat hand and began jerking it back and forth.

"Ye be a sweet young thing, so innocent, so fresh and untouched," Hornby gasped, the red flush on his face increasing, his breath coming in short spurts. "But ye belong to me Master, so I cannot touch ye," he muttered to himself as he jerked the red flesh back and forth. "Oh, but how I want to. Maybe just yer titties..."

He lumbered toward her, his hand jerking faster on the piece of red flesh rising between his legs.

She backed away, but he kept approaching. He was within five feet of her when she felt the far wall of the room touch her back, which meant she could retreat no further. Her attempts to remain calm failed. Terror swept through her, her heart beating wildly, her chest heaving with her agitated breathing. Hornby's eyes glazed over as he stared at her heaving breasts which threatened to burst free from their confines, his hand below his waist moving at a frantic rate.

Suddenly, he let out a loud groan and she saw a whitish fluid squirt out of the red flesh and onto his hand. This seemed to temporarily disable him. He stumbled and looked down at his mussed hand.

Charlotte seized the opportunity to dash around his huge girth and escape the room. She hurried down the hall away from him, still breathing hard, the action further tormenting her nipples. What on earth had just happened, she wondered, determined more than ever to avoid the strange butler in the future.

She wished her mother were there, maybe then she

could ask the questions about male anatomy that had so plagued her in the last few hours. Did Sir Prescott also have such a red thing between his legs? And what was that white substance that had so disabled Hornby? She shuddered at the memory of Hornby's florid face and meaty body, how he had stared at her breasts so hungrily, like a starving man. He had smelled like steak and onions when he had closed in on her.

Taking a deep breath, again aware of how her nipples pressed against the restraints of her bodice, she swung open the door to the parlor.

***

"What do you think, Sally, my dear? Doesn't that gown seem perfect for dinners at Wharton Manse?" Barbara addressed her friend as they watched Charlotte parade in front of them dressed in one of the modiste's latest creations.

At first, Charlotte had felt bashful disrobing in front of the ladies and embarrassed to have so much attention directed toward her. When the modiste had helped her remove her pink gingham and her old corset, both ladies had exclaimed in wonder over the size of her "womanly attributes," as they described her breasts.

"Edmund will thank me for showing those to advantage," Barbara had said as the modiste cinched her into a new and more modern-styled corset.

Charlotte looked in the mirror at the gown she now wore. It was a deep shade of midnight blue, the color subtle, but there was nothing else subdued about it. The material of the skirt was tight and so sheer she could see the outline of her legs through it. Gossamer lace covered the bodice, providing no support for her breasts where they lifted above the tight confines of the corset.

As she turned in front of the mirror, Charlotte could see the hard points of her nipples thrusting against the material and she could swear that the sway of her breasts was also visible beneath the material. No one seeing her in that gown would have any doubts as to the size and shape of her womanly attributes.

She suspected this kind of dress must be the fashion, since Sally had worn such a thing the other night at dinner. But still, the idea of Sir Prescott seeing her dressed in such a garment would be discomfiting, to say the least. And then she suddenly remembered William Hathaway. A deep blush swept up her neck. He had merely rubbed a leg against her last night when she was dressed sedately. How in heaven would a rake such as he be able to restrain himself, if he saw her in this gown?

She remembered seeing him standing between Barbara's legs and suddenly, perversely, imagined he stood between her own legs. Her heart raced and the flush spread higher.

"I do believe our protégé is embarrassed," Sally said, examining Charlotte in the mirror.

"What? Ridiculous! Embarrassed about what?" Barbara peered up at Charlotte. "Gel, whatever is the matter?"

Charlotte turned to the two ladies on the settee. She sought for words to cover her confusion. "I, um, have just never seen such a fine dress."

Sally whispered something to Barbara, who nodded.

"Charlotte, my dear, please walk to that side of the room and then walk toward us," Barbara commanded.

Charlotte wondered why they wanted her to do such a thing, but she complied. At least it distracted her from her errant thoughts. She hunched her shoulders slightly as she walked to help relieve the friction of the bodice against her sensitized nipples.

When she returned to the two ladies, they were whispering together. She only heard the tail end of their conversation.

"You are right, of course," Barbara was saying, a slight

frown on her face. "I want my brother happy, which means William must tutor her. That displeases me, but I agree, it's the only way."

Charlotte knew instinctively they were discussing her, but what did Barbara mean by William tutoring her? She wanted to ask, but she was afraid to reveal she had overheard. They might think her rude for eavesdropping.

The thought of being taught by William terrified her. She suddenly had the image of being alone with him in the library as he lectured her on the geography of Asia. He would probably stand near her, maybe over her as Sir Prescott had when she had lain in bed. Her mouth swept dry, remembering how handsome he was, how manly, and he was a rake. Would there be a chaperone?

"That will be all." Barbara's voice interrupted Charlotte's thoughts. She had risen from the settee and was speaking to the modiste.

"I'll ring for Alice to bring your new garments to your room," Barbara said to Charlotte. "Please make sure to dispose of your old clothing. I am sure you would agree that your fiancé does not want to see you in those old rags." She waved Charlotte toward the door. "We will see you for dinner at seven."

After quickly changing into a new day dress, more sedate than the evening gown, but still form fitting, Charlotte left the room, glad to escape the scrutiny of the two ladies.

***

Having spent a good portion of the day inside, Charlotte thought an exploration of the formal gardens she had seen from her bedroom window would be enjoyable. It was only just five, which gave her an hour for a walk before she would have to dress for dinner. She left her room with trepidation, glancing down each hallway. At all costs, she planned to avoid Hornby the butler.

Unfortunately, she did not know the way to reach the gardens through the massive mansion.

She descended the grand staircase to the first floor, and then guessed that she should head toward the back of Wharton Manse. She heard male voices in the drawing room. Peeking through the door, she saw Sir Prescott and Sir Geary in conversation. She didn't want to disturb their business to ask directions and she did not want company, so she quietly walked past the room and down the hall.

This portion of Wharton Manse was quiet and no one seemed to be about. She wondered if this was the servant quarters, as the hallway had reduced in size and there were no more paintings on the walls. Then, as she moved forward, she heard a thumping noise. It came from one of the rooms up ahead. As she approached, she realized she also heard voices.

"Oh, that's good, gel. Yes, yes," a familiar male voice was grunting.

Charlotte had to pass the room in order to reach the garden. She could see the door to the outside of the mansion dead ahead, but she would have to pass the room, so she slowly crept forward. She couldn't help looking with into the room as she tiptoed past. The sight filled her with fear and consternation.

The room appeared to be a pantry with counters and shelves. Alice stood bent over the counter, her skirts tossed up about her waist, her bottom bare, her thin legs spread wide. Hornby's enormous bulk was pressed up behind the maid and he was moving back and forth against her. His beefy hands were clamped to the Alice s hips. Charlotte noticed his red baton was again protruding from his pants and he was moving it against Alice's bare bottom. As she watched, the baton disappeared into Alice at the same time that the maid made a small moan and Hornby grunted again.

Charlotte hurried past the room, her heart beating in alarm and fear coursing through her. Though she was sure they were too engrossed to notice her pass, she couldn't help thinking about what they were doing, and the thought filled her with trepidation. It all seemed so improper, so incorrect. The sight reminded her of William Hathaway between Barbara's legs, and then she remembered Sir Prescott's attentions to her own body that morning. She felt her body heat with the memories and her breasts tingle. She forced her mind away from such immoral thoughts.

Once outside, she welcomed the cool afternoon air that washed over her heated body as she stepped into the gardens. The rain had gone, leaving the land smelling fresh and cool. The sun sat low in the west. She walked among the hedgerows and thought about Quigley Hall and home.

She wondered how her mother and her two little sisters were faring. How she wished she could speak to her mother about the ways of men and women! She could only hope that Sir Prescott was a gentleman. Reflecting on his behavior to her from the time they first met, she had to admit that he indeed seemed the gentleman. He had always treated her father with respect, and he had offered to care for her family as a condition of his proposal to her, despite the fact that he had kissed her the day of her father's funeral.

She remembered Barbara's comments last night in the parlor. She couldn't help harboring the same question Barbara asked. Why had he proposed to her? Someone of his stature in Society could have made an extraordinary match. Why marry a penniless girl from the country? She wanted to trust him, but without understanding his motives, she couldn't help but be suspicious and apprehensive. He was so much older, so much worldlier, and he had ever so much more experience than she did of pretty much everything.

She looked about her, noticing for the first time that she was walking between a row of high hedges, taller than she. Turning around, she planned to retrace her steps, but then she discovered there were paths leading away on either side of the path she was on. She abruptly realized she was in a maze and that she had gotten herself lost.

"'That's what you get for not paying attention," she said to herself aloud.

"Hallo? Someone there?" A male voice called out somewhere nearby.

Rounding a corner, she found herself face to face with none other than William Hathaway. The surprise of the moment was too much for her. Immediately, she found herself helplessly blushing. He was so tall, so handsome, and they were alone together, hidden in the bushes. She knew him to be a rake, having seen him daily with Barbara, a married woman. Heavens knew what he would do to someone as unschooled in the rules of sensuality as she.

She studied his waistcoat, unable to look up into those intense blue eyes that she felt at that very moment boring into her.

"What do we have here?" He spoke low, his voice deep and resonant, and it sent tremors of awareness through Charlotte's body. She hastily shrank back as he approached, her heart picking up tempo. She feared he might behave with impropriety and then whatever would she do?

"I didn't know that Wharton Manse had a maze, Mr. Hathaway," she said a little breathlessly, forcing herself to stand still when he moved closer. "I thought these were just hedges and then I found myself lost."

William now stood close enough to her that she could smell his fragrant cologne and his appealing male scent. Before she realized what she was doing, she inhaled deeply, drawing in more of his tantalizing scent. He was so unlike Sir Prescott, though they were both quite tall. She could sense his strength, his physical prowess. He was a man in the prime of his life. She couldn't help sympathizing with Barbara. With a husband like Sir Geary, no wonder she had turned to Mr. Hathaway.

She bit back a gasp of surprise when she felt his hand on her chin. He tipped her head up so she was forced to look him in the eyes. She could do nothing but stare helplessly into the most handsome face she had ever seen. His eyes were strikingly blue under a full head of black hair, tied back in a queue. Unwittingly, her eyes fell to his lips as he spoke and she wondered vaguely if he might kiss her.

"I, too, got lost my first time in the maze, but do not fear, Miss Royce, I can take you to safety."

He studied her face and she felt herself blushing under his scrutiny. She wanted to pull her head away from him, and yet she also wondered how it would be if he kissed her. His hand remained firm on her chin.

Afraid to look him in the eye, she stared at his lips. His lips were full and sensuous, his teeth straight and white. Unbidden, she imagined that mouth on her breasts instead of Sir Prescott's. Her blush deepened and to her embarrassment and mortification she felt her nipples pressing hard against the bodice of her day dress. She prayed he would not notice.

William continued to study her face, however, and when he next spoke, it was as though he were speaking to himself. "So young, so innocent. How very refreshing."

Abruptly, he released his hold on her chin and took a step back.

Her eyes flew to his and she realized he was now studying her form, his eyes traveling from her hair, down across her bodice, to her legs and feet. She fought the urge to cross her arms over her chest, knowing he probably could see her erect nipples through the bodice of the day dress.

"Come, Miss Royce, let me now evince your rescue." He held out his arm to her.

She didn't want to appear missish or rude, and he had offered to help her, so she accepted his arm. He tucked her arm against his and led her from the maze.

She knew he was a rake and that for propriety's sake she should avoid him, but as they walked, she couldn't help but revel in the sensation of being alone with such a handsome man. She gripped his forearm and felt the tremendous strength latent in him as he helped her over a rough section of the path.

"How do you like Wharton Manse so far?" he asked politely as they walked.

"It is much more than I ever imagined," Charlotte said. "I wish my mother and sisters could see it. We knew Sir Prescott was a man of standing, but I had no idea—" she broke off, embarrassed, abruptly realizing she sounded mercenary.

"I am sure in time your family will come for a visit," William chuckled, and then added, "If you consider this is opulent, wait until Edmund takes you to London. Aldridge House, his townhouse in the City, is truly magnificent. Of course, if you come to London, I would be honored if you considered paying my family a visit. And I must add, Radway House is every bit as impressive as Aldridge." His voice deepened with pride.

The hedges suddenly gave way, and Charlotte found they had emerged near the front of the house. William escorted her up the flagstone steps to the landing, and she saw that they were now outside the drawing room. Sir Prescott and Sir Geary were inside and saw them.

William turned to her where they stood on the landing, and taking her hand, lifted it to his lips. He bent slightly at the waist and kissed her hand.

"It has been my pleasure to rescue a damsel in distress." His eyes sought hers, and for a moment, she felt as though his piercing gaze had touched her soul.

"Thank-you for your aid," she managed to reply before the drawing room doors opened and she found Sir Prescott by her side.

He immediately took her hand in his. The gesture was

endearing but perhaps also a bit proprietary, and she couldn't help compare the cold boniness of his hand to the warm tensile strength that had run through William's hand and arm where she had touched him.

"How are you, my dear?" Sir Prescott raised Charlotte's hand to his lips and kissed it.

Charlotte tried to respond, but she felt contrite for having compared her fiancé to the young man standing beside them, and then she remembered how Sir Prescott had left her this morning. She felt another flush creep up her neck and again she became aware of her nipples pressing hard against her dress. Momentarily speechless, she studied the buttons of her fiancé's waistcoat.

"I rescued your intended from the maze, Sir. She had become lost within its many paths."

Charlotte was grateful when William spoke up. He then moved up the stairs toward the drawing room. "I must go and prepare for dinner," he said before disappearing inside.

Sir Prescott still held Charlotte's hand. He brought it up to his mouth again, but this time, with his back shielding her from the house, he slipped her finger into his mouth and sucked. She felt his tongue flick against the sensitive flesh between her thumb and index finger.

Charlotte gasped, her eyes fluttering shut. "Sir, what of your guests?" she managed to say.

Sir Prescott did not respond, and Charlotte opened her eyes to see him studying her intently. His eyes traveled over her face and then down to her bosom in the day dress.

"That is better," he murmured. "That is how I want to see you. Now, my dear, go run up and change for dinner. Barbara tells me you have a nice new wardrobe. Indeed, this is a very becoming dress," he said, his hand brushing a glancing caress across her breasts. "Now go," he urged her from him, but not before Charlotte again noticed the protuberance thrusting against his breeches as he turned away from her.

***

Charlotte approached dinner with dread after having to endure Alice's extravagant compliments when she saw Charlotte in her new dinner gown. Her fear was well founded, as she soon discovered. Dressing for dinner in such a gown had taken much longer than expected, so by the time she made her entrance into the dining room, everyone else was in attendance. The reactions of the different parties when they beheld her appearance left her uneasy. On the one hand, Sally looked satisfied, obviously proud of her own power to transform Charlotte from a naive country maid into a Lady of Fashion. Both William and Sir Geary eyed her bosom in a way that reminded her of Hornby the butler's hungry stare. To her surprise, however, both Barbara and Sir Prescott looked angry. Barbara only glanced once at her, before looking away. Sir Prescott stared at her, but rather than look hungry, his lips were compressed in a firm line as he gestured for her to join them.

Rising to his feet, he escorted her to her chair at table.

"You are late," he said under his breath.

"I'm sorry," she said, wanting to apologize and explain about the time it took to don the new dress, but as soon as she saw everyone at the table staring at her, she looked down at her plate and gnawed on her lower lip, wishing she could disappear.

After a few moments, Sir Prescott seemed to relax his mood. "Now that we are all here, I would like to propose a toast," he said and lifted his wineglass. Everyone followed suit, and the servant behind Charlotte hurried to fill her glass with a golden-colored liquid.

"To my bride to be and how happy we all are to have her in our midst."

Charlotte couldn't help blushing at the attention. She

37

was tempted to drink more of the wine, which was surprisingly sweet and delicious, but she remembered what had happened the night before, so she only took a small sip.

Tonight, she was seated beside Sally and so, fortunately, her fears of William and his roving leg were unfounded. But now she found another torment. Whenever she dared to look up from her plate, she felt his blue eyes piercing her from across the table. She swore it was as though his eyes were touching her bosom, tracing the white mounds above the dress, and dipping lower. Imagining his mouth on her breasts and suckling her nipples as Sir Prescott had, she took a shaky sip of wine, knowing her nipples had erected against the gossamer fine bodice.

Suddenly, she felt Sir Prescott's hand cover hers where it rested on the table. He leaned over, his breath warm and moist in her ear. She could smell wine and soup on his breath.

"You look ravishing, my sweet," he whispered, his index finger tracing a pattern across the back of her hand, and then, to her shock, she felt his thin lips nip her ear.

With every ounce of will power, she fought the urge to jump, but she was unable to stop the sweeping blush that covered her face and bosom.

"Love is wonderful to behold." Sir Geary spoke from the other end of the table as he watched them with approbation. "To love," he lifted his glass for another toast, and then he turned to kiss Barbara on the mouth.

Charlotte furtively watched, curious to see Barbara's reaction. To her amazement, Barbara returned Sir Geary's kiss with what looked to Charlotte like believable passion.

She stared back down at her plate, confused. Obviously, her assumption that Barbara did not love Sir Geary must be untrue. It had never occurred to her that a woman might love more than one man. She thought about her feelings for Sir Prescott and William and wondered if perhaps she loved two men, too.

***

Later, when they had removed to the drawing room, while Sally played the piano and Sir Prescott held her hands in a dance, Charlotte wondered if what she felt was actually love. The movement of the dance caused her breasts to swing sensuously against the bodice of her dress and her nipples again had hardened. She hazarded a look up at Sir Prescott and remembered the morning when his mouth had closed over her body so intimately. The memory flooded her body with arousing awareness and she felt the warm wetness seep anew from the juncture of her thighs. Never having been in love, she was uncertain if the sensations she was feeling in her body constituted that emotion. And yet she remembered the scandal novels, which had talked at length about love. Maybe when they described the heroine's heart racing or the thrill she experienced when she encountered her beloved, maybe that was the polite way of describing what Charlotte felt in her body. She wished there was someone she could ask, but looking up into Sir Prescott's debonair and patrician face, she knew she would never have the courage to speak to him about such a thing. He must know how naive she was, but she didn't want to embarrass either of them by drawing more attention to her lack of experience than was absolutely necessary.

As the dance ended, Sir Prescott drew her close, his body pressed to hers. He placed his hands firmly on her hips and pulled her lower body yet closer. She could feel the protuberance pressing into her stomach and she looked up swiftly into his face. His eyes were black and his expression intense, a slight smile curving his thin lips as he stared down past her face to her cleavage, which was now mounded firmly against him. He leaned down.

"A kiss for my intended," he said and then kissed her

on the lips.

Her lips parted in surprise that he would behave so intimately in front of his guests, and her shock increased, when she felt his tongue slip into her parted mouth and brush across her teeth.

Abruptly, she pulled back. "Sir?" she said, unable to stop the flush spreading up her neck as she placed her hands against his chest in an attempt to create some distance between them.

He immediately released her hips and took her hand, bringing it to his mouth. "Excuse me, my dear," he whispered, his expression rueful as he kissed her hand. "Your beauty overwhelms me."

He escorted her to a chair by the fire. Barbara and William danced to the next tune Sally played on the piano.

"Sir Geary, how about that port?" he said to his friend.

Charlotte watched as he and Sir Geary retired to the far side of the room to pour out their drinks. She turned her attention to Barbara and William. She had to admit they were a striking couple. Barbara's dark red hair was set off by the yellow gown she wore and William's tall figure looked dashing in his black dinner suit. Both looked sophisticated, worldly. When the dance brought them alongside her, she noted how Barbara pressed her bosom wantonly against William's chest and how he older woman fluttered her long eyelashes over her striking sherry-colored eyes. Every so often, the tip of her tongue would come out to touch her lips as she darted glances up at William.

Charlotte realized that Barbara was flirting with William, and then it suddenly occurred to her that William was much, much younger than Barbara. Until that moment, she had simply thought of them as mature adults, much older than she, but now she realized that where Barbara was probably in her early forties William was at least ten years younger, perhaps even closer in age to herself.

She studied William's reaction to the older woman's flirtation. A slight smile curved his lips, and his eyes traveled from Barbara's face to her cleavage when she pressed it to his chest. Did he return Barbara's affections, Charlotte wondered. She had, after all, seen them in a dalliance.

And then Sir Prescott returned to her side.

"Come with me for a breath of fresh air," he said, his hand on her bare arm. "I would like a smoke, and for the sake of the other ladies, let us take a turn outside in the cool evening air."

Charlotte nodded, rising to accompany him. As they passed the dancers, her eyes met William's for an instant, and she self-consciously realized he was watching her move across the room, the same slight smile teasing his lips as his eyes traveled avidly across her body.

Outside, the night was cool but not cold. Sir Prescott escorted her to a stone bench at one end of the granite landing and helped her to take a seat. He stood above her, looking down at her, as he lit his cigar.

"I trust, my dear, that you have had a good first day at Wharton Manse?" he asked, inhaling on the cigar.

Charlotte nodded shyly, remembering their morning together and that they were alone together again. Her eyes dropped nervously to his cravat.

As if reading her thoughts, he said, "I know you enjoyed this morning."

Her eyes flew to his, and he smiled.

"I enjoyed it, too." Taking a sip of his port, he continued. "How was the rest of your day? Did you enjoy being fitted for your new wardrobe? I hope my cousin and Sally were helpful to you."

"Oh yes, they were ever so helpful," Charlotte said, beginning to relax in his presence now that it appeared he simply wished to converse. "I would have had no idea what to tell the modiste. I am very grateful for their suggestions." She looked down again at his cravat, her voice dropping with humility. "You know how little experience I have of the world, Sir."

Sir Prescott put his drink on the ledge by the bench and set down the cigar. "My dear, you are my intended. You need not call me Sir," he said, coming close and sitting beside her on the bench. His hand came up and turned her chin to him, forcing her to look into his face.

She nervously drew in a breath and she smelled the pungent scent of tobacco as he moved closer, his thigh pressing against hers, his other hand coming to her bare shoulder and caressing it slightly.

"We are on much too intimate terms for you to call me Sir, my sweet." With those words, he dropped his head and pressed his lips to hers.

She felt his tongue touch her lips, but she was afraid to open her mouth. It had been pleasant enough when he had kissed her earlier, but the thought of a man putting his tongue in hers now seemed strange, even slightly revolting when she imagined tasting the odorous cigar.

He drew his head back and looked down at her, his black eyes intense. "I think it is time for your next lesson," he said, both his hands now caressing her bare shoulders.

The sensation of his hands moving lightly across her skin was distracting, and she shivered with apprehension as she felt her breasts react to his touch as if they had a will of their own.

"I am going to kiss you again, my sweet, but this time, open your mouth to me."

He spoke the words as a command and his mouth swooped down across hers again. He pulled her shoulders closer, pressing her breasts to him. His lips molded hers and his tongue again sought entrance.

She felt bombarded by physical sensations. His body seemed to be everywhere, touching her everywhere, all at once. She gasped as she found herself lifted across his lap and his tongue slipped into her mouth. She tried not to gag from the cigar taste of him, but suddenly, his hands had closed over her breasts, firmly squeezing as his tongue thrust deeply into her mouth. Her heart beat frantically with the assault on her senses and her breathing came fast. Her breasts were on fire where he touched her, throbbing with an inferno of sensation she had never felt before as his fingers plucked her nipples through the bodice of her gown. His tongue continued to dart in and out of her mouth, and she panted under the onslaught. She had no idea a kiss could be so intense, so all encompassing.

"That's right, my sweet, that's good. Yes, very good," Sir Prescott whispered in the brief moments he came up for air, before his mouth descended for another drugging kiss.

He tasted of port and cigars. The flavors were as intense as the kiss and Charlotte shuddered against him. She felt the hard protuberance pressing against her hip but then forgot everything as he pulled her bodice down and freed her breasts to the night air.

"Beautiful," he sighed, staring down at her breasts as he molded them with his hands.

She looked down and saw his darkly veined and bony hands barely containing her overflowing white and unblemished flesh. The contrast startled her, but then his fingers began to pluck her naked nipples, creating an exquisite torment that flowed through her body and she squirmed helplessly on his lap, feeling moisture seep down her thighs. Again she felt the hard thing push into her side.

"That's it, my dear. Feel it, feel how much you desire me," Sir Prescott groaned, his hands now on her hips, as he began to move her against his lap.

The motion thrust the hard thing repeatedly against her hip. His tongue thrust again into her mouth, and Charlotte tentatively touched his tongue with hers. The action seemed to drive him wild. He grabbed her hand and pressed it against the hard protuberance.

"Yes, yes," he grunted, moving her hand rhythmically

along the hard length.

He sunk his head to claim a breast, his lips closing over her nipple, his tongue and teeth inflicting a new torment, even while he moved her hand across the heated protuberance.

Charlotte's head fell back across his arm, her eyes closed as she was overcome by sensation. She couldn't stop the moan that gathered deep in her throat.

"Yes, yes. Feel your desire for me," he muttered before sinking to claim her other breast with his tongue, his teeth and lips.

Her legs moved restlessly across his thighs and the motion seemed to further incite him. He grasped her hand and pushed it inside his breeches, forcing her to wrap it around the moist, heated length of him.

Her eyes swept open with surprise when she felt the hard length of flesh against her palm. Fleetingly, she remembered the butler Hornby and realized that Sir Prescott was having her do to him what Hornby had done to himself, but then her eyes detected a movement at the side of the landing. She froze in dismay. William stood in the shadows, watching them.

"Don't stop now, my dear," Sir Prescott mumbled, moving back up to kiss her on the mouth, his tongue thrusting into hers as his heated length thrust urgently against her palm.

Seeing William was like a bucket of ice water, and Charlotte suddenly felt cold. The situation was embarrassing enough as it was, but she couldn't in good conscience let it continue, not when she knew that William was standing there watching.

She cleared her throat and whispered against Sir Prescott's ear. "There is someone else on the landing, Sir."

Immediately, Sir Prescott withdrew her hand from his breeches and pulled her bodice back up. He smoothly moved her to sit beside him. He rose to retrieve his glass of port and cigar. He took a sip and then puffed on the cigar, standing for a moment with his back to her as he regained his composure and surveyed the gardens.

Charlotte took the opportunity to look for William, but he was no longer there. She wondered how long he watched them and shuddered to think how much he had seen. The idea of him watching Sir Prescott with her was most definitely embarrassing, almost appalling. She imagined what he must have seen, a man almost sixty making violent love to a girl not yet eighteen. The thought unsettled her in the extreme, so she reminded herself of the reasons she was to marry Sir Prescott. He was a good man who had proposed not just to her but who had provided for her family to retain their home. She turned back to her fiancé, noticing the stiff set of his shoulders as he looked out into the night.

Finally, he turned to face her again. His expression was no longer flushed and intense. His eyes swept the landing and then he returned to her side. He took her hand and brought her to her feet beside him. Leaning down, he whispered into her ear. "Did you see who it was, my dear?"

Charlotte knew enough not to admit who she had seen. Instead, she shook her head, again looking at his cravat, too mortified by what he had done to her and that William had seen it to look Sir Prescott in the eye.

"Are you sure you saw someone?" He tipped her head up to his, forcing her to look him in the face.

She blushed deeply, worrying her full lower lip with her teeth as she met his dark stare. She nodded.

"Well, never mind, my dear. We are engaged, after all." Sir Prescott sighed and patted her hand against his. "I suppose it's for the better that we were interrupted. You have a way of making me forget your lesson plan." He smiled, wryly. "My little girl, you have a way of making me forget myself."

He kissed her again briefly, a gentle peck on the lips, and then escorted her back inside.

The rest of the party had retired to places by the fire.

Sir Geary had fallen asleep in the armchair closest to the fire. Sally and Barbara sat on one of the settees. William sat in a chair close to Barbara, leaning against the arm of the settee as he engaged in private conversation with her. When Sir Prescott and Charlotte entered the room, all but Sir Geary looked at them.

Sir Prescott addressed the party. "I hope you have all enjoyed this evening. I am sure I have," he said, smiling and looking down at Charlotte, who couldn't stop the blush heating her cheeks, her thoughts instantly flying to William and that he had watched Sir Prescott with her on the landing.

Both Barbara and Sally giggled at her, and Charlotte wished she were more sophisticated. It was obvious they found her discomfiture amusing. Sir Prescott continued to address the others.

"As you know, I have to go to London tomorrow on business. You are welcome to stay on here at Wharton as long as you like, as I'm sure that my fiancé would like the company. Now, as I will be leaving early tomorrow, my intended and I must bid you good night."

With his hand still holding hers, Sir Prescott escorted her over to the group on the settee. First, he kissed Sally's hand, and then Barbara's.

"Good night," Charlotte said to each of them, trying not to notice how their eyes seemed to read her like an open book and dreading the moment she would have to face William.

When Sir Prescott turned to William, the younger man rose to his feet.

"Mr. Hathaway," he said, shaking William's hand.

"Sir Prescott, it has been a pleasure. And I have particularly enjoyed meeting your charming fiancé," William said, turning to Charlotte.

She felt the deep blue eyes bore into hers, and she hastily dropped her gaze. Before she knew what he was doing, he had taken her hand in his and brought it to his lips.

"Enchanté," he said against her lips.

The sensation of his lips moving over the skin on the back of her hand caused a shimmer of awareness to whisper through her. Fearing Sir Prescott would notice her response, she forced her gaze to the top button of his dinner suit.

"Likewise, I'm sure," she managed to say, her voice fainter than she would have liked.

"Come my dear, it is quite past your bedtime," Sir Prescott said, claiming her hand from William and placing it paternally on his forearm.

Charlotte couldn't help a swift glance up at William. To her surprise, his eyes were on her bosom. She had forgotten how gossamer thin the dress was and realized he was staring at her deep cleavage and her erect nipples where they protruded against her bodice. For some reason, this irritated her. She reminded herself that he was a rake and that rakes behaved improperly. She turned away from him to Sir Prescott.

Outside her bedroom door, Sir Prescott once again enveloped her in a tight embrace.

"I will miss you, my sweet."

His hands wandered down over her hips, pulling her to the hardness against her stomach that was becoming increasingly familiar to her. She felt her nipples grow hard again where they rubbed against his firm chest and she couldn't stop the ripple of awareness from shuddering through her. No one was in the hall watching. She had made sure of that before he had taken her in his arms. Without an audience, she felt free to revel in the wonderful sensations he was evoking in her body. His mouth came down across hers, and this time, when his tongue teased her lips, she opened to him. She no longer found the sensation of his tongue darting in and out of her mouth strange, and it was no longer unpleasant.

He groaned, and against her lips, muttered, "You are

smart, my dear, a quick learner."

Finally, he pulled back, his hands on her bare shoulders, caressing, as he stared down at her, gazing first at her face and then lowering it to her bodice.

"Though it pains me, we will have to postpone your lessons until my return," he sighed.

Charlotte looked up at him, trying to work up enough courage to ask the question that had been plaguing her for months. She nibbled on her lower lip as she looked up at him.

"What is it, my sweet?" The lines on his face showed concern.

"I've been meaning to ask you, Si-" she bit off the word, remembering he had asked her not to use his title. "Sorry," she said, and he smiled, his hand tracing down the side of her face, his thumb coming to rub her full lower lip gently.

"I forgive you, my dear," he breathed. "What is it you've been meaning to ask?"

"Have you set a date for our wedding?"

With that, Sir Prescott laughed. "Are you in a rush to consummate our marriage, my sweet?"

Charlotte looked down, embarrassed. He had misunderstood the reason for her question.

The idea of consummating their marriage had never crossed her mind, but now, the image caused an uneasy tension to flow through her body. Where the idea might have been repulsive just days ago, if she had thought to consider it, she now wasn't so sure. He had taught her things about her body that she had never even suspected, and he had given her a great deal of pleasure. She nibbled her lower lip again, thinking, as Sir Prescott spoke.

"I am a patient man, my dear. As you know, I am a gentleman, and there are rules to observe in order to maintain propriety." Sir Prescott's levity momentarily evaporated and he looked down at her earnestly. "Mourning etiquette dictated the year delay in my proposal, and it is only appropriate that another year pass for our engagement. You are young and I am sure you realize that you need to be schooled for the life you will lead as my wife. I am no hot-blooded youth, impatient for the marriage bed. So, I hope you can stand to wait another year before our wedding night."

Charlotte studied his cravat and nodded, surprised to feel a strong sense of relief sweep through her body that caused muscles she hadn't even known were tense to relax. Maybe she wasn't yet ready to imagine consummating their marriage, after all.

He turned her face up to his again and kissed her firmly on the lips. "I'll be back in a fortnight, my dear. In the meantime, be patient."

He pushed her bedroom door open and then closed it firmly behind her.

*****

3 CHARLOTTE IS TUTORED BY A RAKE

Charlotte slept late the next morning, and when she first arose, she forgot where she was. In the few moments before she opened her eyes, she thought she was back home at Quigley Hall, and she stretched her body languorously among the soft pillows, looking forward to breakfasting with her mother and her sisters.

But then she opened her eyes. As she took in her surroundings, the opulent burgundy velvet bed drapes, the enormous room and ornate furniture, the memories of the previous day flooded through her. She sat up abruptly in bed, hugging her knees to her chest.

She was alone, her family far away, and she was at her fiancé's estate.

Had Sir Prescott really brought her breakfast in bed yesterday morning and had he then kissed her and touched her so intimately?

A brief shudder ran through her. At the time he had touched her, for some reason, she had not found his behavior disturbing. In fact, to be honest, she had almost enjoyed the experience.

Now that she was alone, the memories unsettled her.

As she climbed from the bed, her new nightgown, a

delicate, lacy affair, slid across her breasts and the sensation of her nipples erecting sent a wave of sensual fire through her. Before she knew what she was doing, her hands came up to cup her breasts, much as Sir Prescott had done last night. She gasped as ripples of pleasure poured through her and centered low in her belly. She saw her reflection in the mirror and, with an exclamation of disgust, she hastily removed her hands from herself, suddenly ashamed of her wanton behavior.

She pulled the rope with more force than necessary to ring Alice to come and dress her and then she sat down angrily at the vanity.

What would her mother think of her behavior, she chastised herself. Just a day ago, she had been an innocent, genteel girl from the country. Now, a day later, she had learned things about the male anatomy, much less her own body, that she felt sure was improper for a young girl her age. That thought led her to reflect again on Sir Prescott's behavior. Yesterday, she had convinced herself that he was a gentleman. Now, she frowned as she brushed out her long, blond hair, relishing the punishing pain when she yanked through a knot, she wasn't so sure. He had not behaved as the gentlemen had in the few scandal novels she had read. He had not even given her a bouquet of flowers, something the hero always did in those stories. Instead, he had touched her improperly and manipulated her body most shamelessly for his own pleasure.

She shuddered again at the memory, thinking of his aged hands touching her so intimately.

But then she remembered William and a wave of unwanted heat swept through her.

He is a rake, she told herself, and yet, the thought of him touching her as Sir Prescott had caused her heart to race uncontrollably in her chest.

***

"Oh, there you are, Charlotte. We were about ready to give up hope of seeing you this morning," Barbara said over a cup of tea.

She sat across from Sally at the breakfast table. Without candlelight and a ravishing gown, Barbara looked older. Charlotte noticed in the bright mid-morning light that the other woman's face, though still beautiful, showed her age, worry lines touching the sides of her mouth and her brows.

"I'm sorry. I must have overslept," Charlotte murmured an apology and moved to the sideboard to help herself to the remains of the breakfast.

"The young do need their sleep," Sally smirked.

"Oh be quiet," Barbara snapped.

Charlotte couldn't help looking at her in surprise. Something was definitely bothering the woman. It wasn't polite to pry, so Charlotte pretended to ignore Barbara's unusual behavior and continued spooning scrambled eggs onto her plate.

"I'm surprised at you, Bonnie, really." Charlotte couldn't help but overhear Sally's stage whisper to Barbara. "You were the one who suggested it in the first place. I told you to let him lie in the bed he has made for himself, but you love the poor fool. So stop worrying, it'll all work out just fine."

Barbara bit off her response as Charlotte took her seat at the table. She could feel the tense silence between the other two women and forced herself to nibble on the eggs and toast she no longer desired. She sensed the others studying her, and she made herself sit straight and not hunch self-consciously.

After several uncomfortable moments, Barbara addressed her. "You know that my cousin plans a hunt and an accompanying ball in a fortnight upon his return from London."

Charlotte nodded, remembering the dinner conversation the other night.

"In preparation for the festivities, Sally and I are going into London to shop and procure necessary garments and sundries. Your fiancé has been so generous as to supply us with the funds to buy you clothes and I have your measurements from your fitting yesterday. I will make sure that you have everything you need."

"Thank-you, Barbara," Charlotte said, looking up from her plate as she finished her eggs. She wondered for a moment why they did not include her in their travel plans but then gave up a silent prayer of thanks that she was to stay behind. She would be completely out of her depth on such a trip with two seasoned women of the ton.

The tense expression reappeared on Barbara's face. "My husband also has business in the City and will accompany us. In order that you do not feel lonely being left all alone here at Wharton Manse, Mr. Hathaway has kindly agreed to stay on."

Sally tittered at that last statement, and Barbara shot her an angry glare before continuing. "We will return before the end of the week and will then ready the house for the guests."

"The hunt sounds interesting." Charlotte forced herself to think about the week ahead and not the next few days when she would be alone at Wharton Manse with William Hathaway, a hopelessly handsome rake.

"Sir Prescott puts on great parties," Sally smiled. "He's expecting upwards of twenty guests, isn't that so, Bonnie?"

The other woman nodded, studying Charlotte pensively as she finished her tea and rose to her feet. Sally followed suit.

"We will see you in a few days," Barbara said.

"Hope you don't find it too dull around here," Sally smirked before following Barbara from the room.

Charlotte stared out into the sunlit garden. The beauty of the day and the blooming flowers weren't able to lessen the sense of foreboding she felt. It was one thing to entertain a whimsical, girlish fantasy about William. It was quite another to think about the reality of being forced to endure the company of a confirmed rake in solitude without the benefit of a chaperone.

She worried her full lower lip between her teeth. Barbara had seen fit to dally with William, even as a married woman. But Charlotte wasn't married yet. She thought of Sir Prescott and his promise to help her family as part of his marriage contract to her. Even if she had been tempted to form a dalliance with the William, in good conscience, she could not betray her commitment to Sir Prescott.

She may be naive, but she wasn't stupid. She knew that if she were caught alone with William, she would be at his mercy. So the question became, how she could avoid his company for the next couple of days?

She stood from the table and headed back upstairs to her room. Much as she wanted to explore more of Wharton Manse, and in particular the beautiful gardens, she knew her presence alone in public was too risky. She would have to remain confined to the safety of her room, at least until the return of Barbara and her friend. She turned the key in the lock and breathed a sigh of relief when she was once again ensconced in her room.

***

The sun had arced passed noonday when she stood on the balcony of her second floor room, enjoying the warmth of the sun on her face and limbs and watching the Geary carriage roll away down the long gravel drive and disappear into the forest. Her eyes strayed down to the gardens. Abruptly, she noticed William standing not far below her at the beginnings of the maze. He was staring intently up at her. Even from that distance, she could feel his eyes raking her form. Hastily, she withdrew into the privacy of her chambers, sorry to lose the enjoyable sensation of the sun warming her skin but relieved to no longer feel his scrutiny.

She sat down at the small writing table and began work on a letter to her family. Some time later, a knock sounded on the door.

"Come in," she said.

The doorknob jiggled. She forgot she had locked it.

"Just a minute." She hurried to the door. Remembering her predicament, she asked, "Who's there?"

"It's me, Alice, the maid, Miss."

"Oh, please come in." Charlotte unlocked the door and opened it.

"Luncheon be served downstairs, Miss."

"I would prefer to take my lunch in my rooms. I hope the staff hasn't gone to too much trouble for me."

Alice frowned, but then nodded. "Tis simply cold cuts, Miss Charlotte."

"Good. Would you be willing to bring me a plate?"

Alice nodded and headed for the door.

"One more thing, Alice," Charlotte added. "Can you please inform the cook that I intend to take all my meals in my room until the Gearys return."

Alice looked at Charlotte in surprise. "If ye don't mind me askin', ye be feeling OK, Miss?"

"Yes, perfectly fine, thank-you. I have several matters I must attend to here." Charlotte waved vaguely toward the writing table where her letter home still lay.

Alice clucked her tongue as she left the room, saying, "Mr. Hathaway will be none too happy about this."

***

Early the next morning, Charlotte paced the room, feeling like she would go mad with boredom.

She had written her letter yesterday. Indeed, she had proceeded to write individual letters to each of her sisters, too. Then, she had read the one book she had found in the room, a hopelessly boring work of ancient Roman history.

Starved for company by evening, she had tried to strike up a conversation with Alice when the maid brought her dinner up on a tray. The maid had been taciturn, obviously uncomfortable speaking familiarly to someone above her station. Goaded partly out of frustration from Alice's lack of response and partly out of curiosity, Charlotte had questioned the maid about her relationship with Hornby, the butler.

"What do ye mean, relationship?" Alice had demanded, forgetting servant etiquette, a flush spreading across her cheeks.

"You know what I mean," Charlotte had said, a small smile touching her lips, but privately wishing she could retract the question. She felt a blush stain her own cheeks and realized she was as embarrassed at asking the question as the maid was in answering.

"I don't see how it be any business of yourn, Miss," Alice said, as she completed the place setting on the small table by the window.

"You're right. I apologize. I didn't mean to pry." Charlotte breathed a sigh of relief to let the matter drop.

Before closing the door to Charlotte's room, Alice made a final parting request. "I ain't admitting to nothin', Miss, but I'd appreciate it if ye don't mention me affairs to anyone, 'specially the Master and his cousin."

She had agreed.

Now, she pushed the curtains aside so she could look out at the garden. It was another gorgeous spring morning, the sun shining warmly in a clear blue sky. The winter had been long, cold and dark. How she wanted to go outside and enjoy the day! She remembered her encounter in the garden with William. Going out of doors was too dangerous. She let the curtain fall and returned to pacing the room, wondering how on earth she could pass the time. She looked at the clock on the mantle. It was not yet eight o'clock. She thought about the library she had passed the other day when she had gone into the gardens. If she could pick up a few books, the time spent in her room would be less tedious. It was still quite early. Maybe if she hurried she could sneak down to the library undetected. If William's habits were like the other guests at Wharton Manse, he wouldn't rise before ten.

She shrugged out of her nightgown. There was no time to call Alice to help her don her corsette. Instead, she simply slipped on one of the day dresses that buttoned up the front. Unlike most of the other dresses Barbara had procured for her, this one was one she could button herself. It was also one of the most modest with a high neckline.

Her heart beat rapidly as she turned the lock on the door and swung it slowly open. She held her breath and listened as she looked down the hallway in each direction. Besides the ticking of the grandfather clock at one end of the hall, everything was quiet. She tiptoed as fast as she could to the head of the grand staircase, fearing that at any moment, she might encounter Hornby the butler or even William himself. Suddenly, another servant appeared below her in the main hall carrying a tray. She flattened herself against the wall and held her breath, praying he would not look up to where she stood. When he disappeared from view, she couldn't help but give a little sigh of relief. Not wasting any more time, she flew down the stairs and around the corner. The coast was clear and she beelined for the library door. Hurriedly, she pulled it open, ducked inside and closed it quietly behind her.

"How good of you to join me for breakfast, Miss Royce."

Charlotte spun around to find the servant she had seen earlier now pouring out tea for William Hathaway, who sat in a comfortable chair by the window, a breakfast service set on the table in front of him. His long legs were encased in casual tan trousers. He wore boots and he was in his shirtsleeves, the neck open just enough to reveal curling dark chest hair. She couldn't help but stare, her mouth suddenly dry, her mind running through possible excuses for how to escape.

"Dalton, can you please lay another service for Miss Royce," William instructed the servant.

"But of course, sir," the man said, nodding as he passed Charlotte.

She jumped when she heard the door close behind her, realizing that her worst fears had just come true. She was alone with a rake.

William rose. Charlotte found herself helplessly backing away from him, staring at his dangerously attractive, tall and lithe form as he approached, until she felt the doorknob jam into her back.

"There really is no reason for you to look like a startled deer trapped in a hunter's sights," William laughed, his voice deep and resonant. He held out his arm. "Come and breakfast with me. There is no harm in that, surely?"

Charlotte looked at his arm, worrying her full lower lip between her teeth, her mind frantically trying to decide what to do. She feared he was laughing at her. She worried he might find her naive, girlish and silly, nothing like the worldly sophistication of Barbara and the others. Was he making fun of her? She risked looking up into his penetrating deep blue eyes. To her surprise, he was smiling encouragingly without any trace of mockery. Relief swept through her.

"Come on, I won't bite," he said as he proffered his arm.

She took a deep breath and finally relented to his request, placing her hand on his arm. He escorted her to the table and settled her in the chair across from his.

"There, that wasn't so bad, was it?" he said, resuming his seat and facing her across the small table.

She nodded, studying the pattern in the tablecloth. She

was too embarrassed by the intimacy of the setting to look at him directly, but she could feel his eyes on her. She was thankful for the modest dress, though without the corset, she knew that her breasts moved more freely beneath the garment. She wondered if he were looking there. She cursed the blush heating her cheeks at her thoughts, but not for anything would she risk glancing up to see where he looked.

Out of the corner of her eye, she saw him pick up his cup of tea and take a sip. The silence lengthened uncomfortably, but she had no idea what to say to the man, and as long as he continued studying her as he was doing, her mind refused to help her out.

The sound of Dalton entering the room with another breakfast setting broke the silence. The servant smoothly set her place, presenting her with toast, eggs, sausage and ham.

"Thank you, Dalton," William said. "That will be all."

The servant left as smoothly as he had entered, and Charlotte found herself once again alone with William.

"Would you like some tea?" he asked politely.

She nodded and couldn't help admiring how gracefully such large hands could manage the delicate china.

"If I didn't know better, I would think you've been trying to avoid me."

With his words, Charlotte sputtered on her mouthful of tea. Instantly, William was behind her, patting and rubbing her back. She held her napkin to her mouth, gasping for air and blushing beet red. When she was finally able to breath normally again, she found him still standing above her. He took her chin in his hand and lifted her face to his.

"Are you feeling better?"

She nodded and couldn't help but be touched by his concern. So far, he had behaved as the perfect gentleman, and she had acted missishly.

"Yes, thank you." Her eyes met his and she fought the

desire she felt pulling her toward his exquisite masculine beauty. She found herself unable to stop staring into his beautifully blue eyes and then at his sensual lips, so unlike her fiancé's thin ones.

His large hand came up and brushed a strand of long blond hair back from her face.

"Good, I am glad."

Charlotte wasn't sure but that she was disappointed when he took his seat again at the table. She was appalled for a moment that she had imagined those remarkable lips against her own. She looked down blankly at her breakfast, her appetite gone. She wasn't prepared to tell him the truth, but at least she owed him an explanation for her reclusive behavior.

Taking a sip of tea to wet her dry throat, Charlotte spoke. "Mr. Hathaway, I meant you no disrespect. You must know that I have led a sheltered country life and as such I am not used to conversing with people outside my family circle. I must confess that I have been intimidated coming to Wharton Manse." Her eyes met his fleetingly before she looked back down at her tea. "My first few days here have been unsettling."

She finished her cup of tea and placed it on the table. William rose and she eyed him warily as he came over and pulled back her chair.

"I understand completely, Miss Royce." His voice was sympathetic. "Wharton Manse can seem sometimes like a museum, maybe even a mausoleum," he laughed. "Here, let us sit more comfortably on the settee."

His hand on her arm, she found herself seated next to him on a red velvet settee. His thigh was not quite touching the fabric of her dress. He leaned back against the settee, clasping his hands behind his head. The action served to pull wider the opening at the neck of his shirt. Her eyes traveled unwittingly to the crisp hair revealed there. She wondered what it would feel like to touch. He stretched out his long booted legs, which pushed the material of his tan trousers taut across his groin. Her eyes sank lower and she wondered about the baton of flesh she knew to be hidden there.

Abruptly, she realized he was watching her. Her eyes flew up to his and she felt another blush begin to heat her cheeks. She tore her gaze away to stare blindly across the room at the bookshelves. From the corner of her eye, she saw one of his arms come to lie atop the back of the settee. Her pulse quickened. If he reached forward, his hand would be in her hair.

"Your engagement will give you time to grow accustomed to the opulence of Wharton Manse. You must realize that once you become Sir Prescott's wife, all that you see here will be under your domain. Indeed, you will be expected to oversee the running of the place."

"If you're trying to help me feel less intimidated, I'm not sure it's working." Charlotte forced a small smile.

She felt the settee dip as William moved closer to her. His thigh now contacted her skirt, indeed, she could feel the hard length of it pressing into the softness of her own leg. Her heart fluttered, but she wasn't sure if it was fear or anticipation. Would he take advantage of the situation? She felt his hand brush the back of her head.

"I can think of one way to help you feel less intimidated." His words came low, his voice deepening.

She felt his hand in her hair, forcing her to turn her head to him. With his other hand, he cupped her chin, and she found herself helplessly looking up into his sensual face, his lips only inches from hers. She tried to remain calm, but it was impossible. Her heart beat like a wild thing in her chest, her breath coming quickly.

"Sir?" she managed to say.

A knock at the door interrupted the moment.

"Come," William called out, rising smoothly to his feet and going to open the door to the library.

Dalton reappeared. "The dishes, Sir," he said.

"Of course." William stood by while Dalton collected

the breakfast things.

Charlotte realized that this was her chance for escape. She pushed off the settee, surprised to feel how languid her legs felt.

"One moment, Miss Royce, if you please," William said before she had gone two paces. "I would like one more word with you before you leave."

Charlotte wasn't sure what to say, since Dalton was still collecting the trays and she didn't want to make a scene.

She nodded, feeling as though her fate had just been sealed. As Dalton left the room, she heard the key turn in the lock. Her eyes flew to his. A slight smile curved his lips. His eyes glinted and she could swear she saw the glimmering of that same masculine hunger she had seen before. She found herself backing away from him, and to her surprise, her action seemed to cause the look to intensify.

"Miss Royce, as I have said, I mean you no harm. You have told me you feel intimidated by Wharton Manse and all that it signifies and that you are concerned about what lies in store for you as Lady Prescott, Earl of Wharton. My only desire is to help you adapt to your new environs and perhaps help you overcome some of that fear."

His words sounded calm, logical, as though he were providing a simple argument, but the look in his eyes caused Charlotte's mouth to go dry. She worried her lower lip between her teeth as he approached, but when that didn't work, she resorted to wetting her lips with her tongue.

The action seemed to spark a fire in his eyes and he moved resolutely toward her. She found herself backed against the bookshelf in the corner of the room. He had effectively trapped her. There was nowhere to go. She was unable to tear her eyes from his, even as his dropped to take in her lips and then dropped lower to travel over her bosom and slowly down the stretch of her body.

"Yes, Miss Royce, I assure you, I only have your best

interests at heart." With those words, his hand came out to flick open the top button of her dress.

Charlotte gasped, her hands instinctively coming up to stop him, but before she thought of the consequences of her actions, her hands had touched his where it rested on the second button of her dress. With a gasp, she dropped her arms, unprepared for the wildfire that coursed through her the moment she had touched his big, warm hand.

Dragging her eyes from his face, she made the mistake of looking down and his riding pants. Something swelled and thrust toward her through the tight tan material.

"Relax, Miss Royce. You are much too tense."

His hand had released two more buttons, but then stopped. Her neck was now exposed where the dress hung open. Both his hands came up to caress her shoulders.

"Here, this should help you relax."

Charlotte felt his hands firm on her shoulders as he propelled her to turn away from him. She faced the bookcase as his large, powerful hands began to work magic on her tense shoulders and neck. For a moment, she forgot the impropriety of the situation, that she was alone with a rake. All she could focus on was the wonderful, bone-melting magic his hands were working on her shoulders and upper back as he kneaded her muscles. Her eyes closed and she couldn't help release a deep shuddering breath.

"That's better," his voice came low and deep behind her. She felt it stir the hair on the back of her neck.

Suddenly, she felt his lips on her ear. She immediately began to tense again, but then his hands resumed their methodical rubbing of her shoulders.

"Yes, let it go," he spoke softly into her ear, causing frissons of reaction to sweep through her body and she felt her nipples erect against the loose material of her dress.

Again she felt his lips on her ear, but this time, she couldn't fight the pleasure. She sighed.

"Yes, very good," he whispered, his tongue tracing the curve of her ear.

More shivers of awareness rippled through her. His hands rested on her shoulders, no longer massaging her. A different kind of tension began to grow in her. Heat began to pool low in her belly. His lips dropped to the side of her neck, exposed by the unbuttoned top of her dress. When she squirmed, he held her shoulders firmly with his hands and she felt his teeth delicately nip at her neck.

"Sir!" She couldn't help exclaiming as the sensations ripped through her.

The feel of his big hard hands on her shoulders, his mouth on her neck, was driving her wild. She couldn't believe it, but she actually wanted him to take her breasts in his hands as Sir Prescott had done. For a moment, she felt shame, desiring another man beside her fiancé to touch her, but then the urgent demands of her body pushed away the thought. She felt the heavy weight of her breasts, where they hung freely without the artificial confines of the corset, her nipples diamond hard, throbbing.

"Yes?" his sibilant whisper caused another shimmer of sensation to sweep through her.

"Please," she gasped, realizing the situation was flaring out of control. "Please stop," she tried to clarify, but even she could hear how much her voice lacked conviction, her words not more than a throaty whisper.

"Of course," came his answer, and to her surprise, his hands instantly left her shoulders and he removed his lips from the side of her neck. She felt rather than heard him move away from her, the air cooling in his absence.

Her fingers flew to the buttons of her dress, fumbling as she rebuttoned them. Taking a deep breath, she forced herself to turn around.

William leaned against the window looking out into the garden.

"I'm sorry," she said, and then instantly wished she

could retract the apology.

It wasn't as if she had done anything wrong. He was the one who had overstepped the bounds of propriety.

He looked toward her, the predatory gleam in his eye replaced by a friendly light. "Miss Royce, you owe me no apology, of that, I am sure. I merely wanted to help you relax and not feel so intimidated here at Wharton Manse. That continues to be my goal."

He pushed away from the window and approached her, claiming her hand. Bending slightly at the waist, he pressed his lips to the back of her hand and gave it a chaste, gentlemanly kiss. She fought the quiver of awareness that raced up her arm and set her body on fire again.

He stood looking down at her, an elegant and dangerously attractive specimen of manhood.

"I understand if you would like some time to yourself," he said. "But you would do me a great honor if you would join me for dinner tonight."

She risked looking up into his blue eyes. She could detect nothing there but what looked to be a sincere offer of friendship. She was tempted to refuse, afraid of her own inability to control herself or at least her errant thoughts around him, but realized how rude, how childish, that would be. If she were really to become Lady Prescott of Wharton Manse one day, she should be able to dine with a gentleman, even if the man were a rake. And, it was not as if he had forced himself on her, she had to admit.

"It would be my pleasure, Mr. Hathaway," she said, but hoped she would not regret it.

He nodded, and then turning on his booted heel, went to unlock the door of the room.

"Until this evening, then," he said and disappeared out into the hall.

***

Shakespeare fell to her lap as Charlotte gazed out the window of her bedroom toward the garden. She had come to the limits of her ability to force herself to focus on the play and not think about what had transpired earlier.

She put the book down and went to open the doors to the balcony. The afternoon air had cooled, and she felt a refreshing breeze waft over her body. She leaned against the balustrade and looked out over the garden, thinking of breakfast. William had behaved for the most part like a complete gentleman. She thought of how kindly he had served her tea and how considerate he had seemed about her introduction to Wharton Manse. Of course there was the moment he had unbuttoned her dress. She remembered the feel of his hands on her, rhythmically rubbing her shoulders, and then his lips on her ear, her neck. She squirmed and shook her head, trying to banish her thoughts of William by thinking of her fiancé. She tried to remember Sir Prescott and his tender ministrations, but to her disgust, all she could do was fantasize about how it would have felt if William had touched her breasts instead.

She frowned, wondering how was she going to get through dinner with him.

At least she was no longer so afraid of him. She looked down at the garden and thought that maybe a walk would help soothe her mind. She had seen him ride out earlier on a great black horse, so she thought it likely to be safe for a visit to the garden.

As she walked down the hall, she suddenly saw a bulky figure shadowed against the bright outside light of the open garden door. In her worry about William, she had completely forgotten about Hornby the butler. His huge bulk blotted out most of the light streaming in from the garden doorway.

"Ah, Miss Royce, ye be lookin' nice today." He advanced on her.

Charlotte had learned enough in the last few days to know that if she were to retreat from him she would reveal her fear and, as experience had taught her, this seemed to incite men, so instead, she stood her ground. She couldn't help contrasting his appearance to William's. Where William was tall, lean, and seductively handsome, Hornby was short, fat and absolutely revolting. She forced herself to remain where she was, though she couldn't stop her heartbeat from accelerating. He came so close she could smell his hot breath on her face and his enormous gut almost touched the front of her dress.

"Ye be lookin' real nice." His thick red lips slobbered over the last words, and she shuddered to see a little saliva drool down into his beard.

Suddenly, she felt his sweaty, meaty hand clamp her breast and squeeze.

She was so shocked that for a second she could do nothing but stand there and stare down at his hand on her, convulsively squeezing her flaccid breast.

"Hallo, what's goin' on here?"

A woman's voice caused her to jump back from Hornby, embarrassment heating a blush across her cheeks. Alice stood with her hands on her hips, looking back and forth between the two of them, accusation in her eyes.

"It's not what you think, Alice," she said, crossing her arms against her chest and trying to sound authoritative.

Unfortunately, she remembered how she had questioned Alice the night before, and it was obvious that Alice thought she and Hornby were having an affair. If the idea weren't so appalling, it would have made her laugh.

"I am going to the gardens." She stepped around Hornby, who was reaching for Alice.

Before she stepped outside, she couldn't resist looking back over her shoulder. Hornby had Alice by the hand and was dragging her into one of the servant's rooms. Charlotte was pretty sure what was going to happen next.

Instead of dwelling on that disgusting thought, she bent over to smell one of the early roses. The sweet fragrance washed all the improprieties from her mind. She was tired of thinking about the ways of men and women. For a moment, she just wanted to be a girl again. She avoided the maze, not wanting to risk getting lost. Instead, she headed into the flower garden and reveled in being outside in the fresh open air. As she walked, she thought of her family and wondered how they were doing at Quigley Hall.

***

The afternoon had grown humid, and when Charlotte found herself at the edge of the vast wood and game lands that bordered the Wharton properties, she thought the cool of the forest might be refreshing. The path she had been following led into the wood. She cast a quick glance at the sky. It was true that a few clouds had gathered, but they looked puffy and innocent enough. Looking at the sun's location, she guessed it to be not yet four o'clock. She heard the tinkle of a stream coming from somewhere inside the forest, the refreshing sound of which beckoned her.

Stepping out of the sun and into the cool shade of the forest was welcome relief. Shortly along the path, she came to the brook. It burbled happily against the stones along its banks. Charlotte looked about. Confirming her privacy, she slipped off her shoes and, taking a seat on a larger rock by the stream, dipped her feet into the brook. The feel of the cool water running over her feet felt delicious, and she sighed, leaning back against the rock and enjoying the quiet beauty of the place.

She must have dozed off, because the next thing she knew, she felt a pair of strong hands on her right foot, massaging it. Maybe it was because she wasn't fully awake but the sensation felt surprisingly good. One of the hands began to creep up above her ankle and her eyes flew open in shock.

"William!" she exclaimed and tried to pull her leg from his grasp.

When she saw his sensual lips curve up in a smile and the intensity of his expression, she realized she had addressed him by his Christian name. She felt the blush sweep across her cheeks.

"I mean, Mr. Hathaway. What are you doing?"

She tried once more to remove her leg from his grasp. It was impossible. He was too strong. He knelt beside her in riding clothes, though he had discarded his coat. His white linen shirt hung open at the neck, a sharp contrast to his dark chest hair. Nearby, the tethered black horse cropped the tender grass that grew beneath the forest canopy.

"Miss Royce, or should I call you Charlotte? I am honored that you think of me in such familiar terms."

He removed one of his hands and she hastily tucked her left leg back under the hem of her skirt. He kept a firm hand on her right foot, and her brows swept up in surprise when he picked up one of her shoes and a stocking.

"You have beautiful feet," he said, as he leaned forward and slipped the stocking onto her foot.

He slid it up her leg. Her breath caught in her throat as she felt his hands on the sensitive area behind her knee. The action of pulling the stocking on felt like a caress. Her eyes swept to his face, but his expression was shielded by the lock of black hair that had fallen across his brow. He tightened the garter band below her knee and she thanked heavens that she had worn low stockings for her walk in the gardens. The thought of his hands on her upper thighs caused a wave of heat to sweep through her. He slid on her shoe.

"May I have the other?" He held out his hand toward the foot she had hidden under her skirt.

She felt his devilishly attractive eyes on her face, but

she kept her head down. She stared at the hand he held out toward her. It was large, graceful, and she knew it was strong. She fleetingly remembered the feel of it on her shoulders and neck this morning, and then on her feet, creating such delicious sensations in her body. He had magic hands.

As she stared, she worried her lower lip between her teeth, reasoning with herself. Finding her alone in the secluded setting, he could easily have ravished her. Instead, he had only behaved mildly improperly. And now, he simply wanted to put on her shoe.

She let out a breath and then withdrew her bare foot from the safety of her skirt. So far, Mr. Hathaway had behaved more the gentleman than the rake. She decided she was being rude as well as missish to distrust him so blindly. Based on his behavior, her fears appeared to be mostly unfounded.

"Of course, and thank-you, Mr. Hathaway," she said.

Just as he cinched the garter in place, a clap of thunder caused them both to jump. The horse neighed, rearing its head back, and within seconds, large raindrops began to fall.

William didn't waste any time. Quickly placing the shoe on her foot, he helped her to her feet.

"Come, Miss Royce. If we are lucky, we will be able to outrun the storm."

He shrugged into the riding coat and gripped her arm. Before she realized what he was about, she found herself swung up onto the horse.

"But, Mr. Hathaway, I don't know how to ride," she exclaimed, grasping frantically at the horse's mane in terror of falling. The ground looked so far away.

William sprang up behind her on the horse.

"Don't worry, I will show you how to ride." His voice suddenly sounded in her ear, startling her.

She gasped as she felt his muscular arm wrap around her waist and draw her back against his solid form.

Looking down, she saw how his long, hard thighs pushed into hers, encompassing her. She felt the hard heat of his body against her back, his breath warm against her ear, and his arm was like a steel band, pulling her firmly against him. The saddle pressed against a sensitive place between her legs, and as he urged the horse forward, she bit back a cry of surprise at the sensations that coursed through her. For some reason, she felt her breasts erect against her dress and warmth pooled between her legs.

The rain began to fall in earnest.

"Wharton Manse is not too far. If we hurry, we shall not get soaked," William spoke in her ear. "Hold on tight to Champion's mane."

She nodded, unable to speak as tension built in her belly. He squeezed his legs against Champion's flanks, pressing the saddle more fully against her, and suddenly Charlotte felt like she was flying. The black horse flew over the path, out of the forest and toward the stables at the back of Wharton Manse. The tension flared hotter and higher between her legs, the saddle pushing rhythmically against the junction of her thighs, William's body pressing into hers from behind, the arm he had tucked around her just inches below her breasts. She wasn't sure how much more she could take. It felt as if at any moment something would snap.

And then they were under the dry roof of the stables, William's hands on her waist, helping her down. She swayed on her feet, her legs feeling rubbery, her body trembling with sensation. William placed his hands once more on her waist.

"Careful, Miss Royce. Are you feeling unwell?" He stood within inches of her, looking down at her, his big hands firm on her waist.

Her body pulsed in strange places and she felt her nipples pressing against the wet material of her bodice. She was afraid to look up at him, sure he could see through the material of her dress. Her face was eye level with the opening of his shirt, and she found herself staring at his black chest hair in fascination, wondering absently how it would feel to run her hands through it. A stable boy appeared and whisked Champion away.

"Miss Royce?" William repeated the question.

Charlotte shook her head, angry at her errant thoughts. She made to pull away from him, and his hands instantly released their hold on her.

"I have never ridden before, Mr. Hathaway. I was unprepared for the experience."

"A fast ride can be an exhilarating experience, Miss Royce. I am glad to have had the honor of introducing you to the pleasures of riding."

Something about the quality of his voice caused her to look up. He was smiling, but there was a predatory glint in his eye as he looked at her. His gaze wandered slowly over her body before returning to her face, and she self-consciously crossed her arms over her chest, not realizing that the action pulled the material even tauter against her erect breasts. The gleam in his eye intensified and he held out his arm to her.

"Come, let us return to the house so we may change out of these wet clothes."

They dashed across the short distance from the stables to the house, and he escorted her up the grand staircase. As they approached her room, her heart fluttered in consternation at the thought that he might now take advantage of her. Impatient with herself, she repressed her overactive imagination. He opened the door to her bedroom but did not accompany her inside. Instead, he stopped on the threshold.

"I have greatly enjoyed your company this afternoon, Miss Royce. You would do me a great honor if you would join me for dinner tonight," he said and took her hand in his.

Bringing it to his lips, he turned it over. She felt a shiver of response pulse through her from her fingers all the way to her toes at the feel of his sensual lips against the sensitive skin of her palm. And then he released her hand. She looked up at him. His blue eyes were burning, his face a study in masculine perfection. He was dangerous and exciting and she didn't want to spend another boring night alone in her room.

She nodded at him. "Yes, Mr. Hathaway, I will have dinner with you."

The white flash of his smile jolted through her. Her worries and her fears evaporated, and she found herself looking forward to the evening with anticipation.

***

As Alice cinched up her corset, Charlotte studied her reflection in the floor length mirror. No longer in William's stimulating presence, some of her concerns had returned. Both this morning and this afternoon when William had seen her, she had been garbed in modest clothing. What if when he saw her in the revealing dinner gown tonight he lost his head? But then she reminded herself to stop being so naive. Her outfit was no more revealing than those Barbara and Sally had worn at dinner the other nights. She herself may not be accustomed to such clothing, but surely Mr. Hathaway as a member of the ton had seen more than his share of revealing gowns.

Alice helped her don the gown with admiration. "Very nice, Miss. That is a fine dress, much nicer then them ones ye brought with you when you arrived."

She looked at the blue satin gown, its color mirroring her eyes. As with the other dinner gowns Sir Prescott had provided her with, this one also had a plunging neckline and a fitted waist that showed off her figure admirably.

"Yes. Sir Prescott has been very generous with me," she said.

As she descended the grand staircase to the drawing room, she briefly wondered if dining alone with William would be considered improper since she was engaged to Sir Prescott. Would she be dishonoring her engagement to Sir Prescott? It was not too late. She could plead a headache and escape to the safety of her room. But then she remembered the comment Barbara had made about her needing company. Surely, William must be here at Sir Prescott's command, and the idea of spending another lonely night in her room was unappealing, to say the least.

She thought of her impending marriage to Sir Prescott, but the more she thought of her fiancé, the more she couldn't help but compare him with William, the most handsome, attractive and exciting man she had ever met. She knew her destiny lay in marrying the older man, but she couldn't help selfishly wanting to spend a little more time in William's company. The Gearys would be back in a day and the opportunity would be gone, probably forever. Her fate would be sealed and she would marry Sir Prescott. So, why not have dinner with William? Besides, she reasoned, how much harm could come from a dinner with the man? At least she would have the memories to cherish in the years to come once she was bound in matrimony to Sir Prescott.

***

Hornby greeted her at the bottom of the stairs. To her relief, he behaved decorously, except for perhaps an overly long stare at her bosom. He escorted her to the drawing room and opened the door.

"Miss Royce, sir," he announced and then removed himself from the room, closing the door softly behind him.

Charlotte heard the latch click and saw William approach her from the other side of the room.

"Enchanté, Miss Royce." William's blue eyes traveled over her body with a potency that caused her to drop her gaze in embarrassment. "You look ravishing," he said and claimed her hand, turning it over so he could place a lengthy kiss on her palm.

His words were as distracting as the feel of his sensual lips on her skin.

"Sir, do you intend to ravish me?"

She could have kicked herself the instant the breathless words left her lips. She could feel the blush heat her face, though she didn't know it also pinkened the snowy flesh exposed by her low décolletage. William smiled as he straightened, keeping a firm grip on her hand. She felt him staring down at her, but she was mortified by the question she had asked. He must think her a silly and naive country girl with no tact. With his other hand, he raised her chin and forced her to meet his gaze.

In the candlelight of the drawing room, his eyes were dark wells of mystery, half hidden in shadow by the lock of black hair that fell across his brow. She couldn't help admiring the masculine beauty of his face, the sharp lines of his cheekbones and jaw made the more dramatic by the sensual curve of his lips and his classic patrician nose. Though his lips were quirked in the slightest of hint of a smile, his expression was not amused. Instead, she sensed an intensity about him that set her heart racing and her breathing to falter.

"Miss Royce, I have no intention whatsoever of ravishing you, despite how pleasurable that experience would be for the both of us, I am sure."

Before continuing, he guided her to the settee near the fire and then went to pour them both sherries. She found herself unable to keep from watching, admiring his tall, lean form move about the room. The black formal dinner suit fit him perfectly, emphasizing the long lines of his legs, and the snowy white cravat provided a crisp and pleasing contrast to the blackness of his hair and outfit. He returned with the sherries and settled himself beside her on the settee.

"Before our evening together continues, you must

understand a few things," he said.

She was afraid to look him in the eye, afraid of what she might see in his face and of what she might show him in her own. Instead, she studied how such a large and masculine-looking hand could so delicately enclose the petite crystal sherry glass within its strong embrace. She watched entranced as he brought the crystal to his lips and took a sip.

"Miss Royce, I am a second son. My older brother, Simon, stands to inherit everything. When our father dies, he will become the next Earl of Radway."

She took a sip of her sherry as she listened, intrigued to consider that William had a brother. She wondered if Simon shared his brother's incredible good looks.

"How unfortunate for you, Mr. Hathaway," she murmured.

"I neither want nor need your sympathy, Miss Royce. The reason I tell you this is so that you understand how grateful I am to your fiancé, Sir Prescott. A year ago, I experienced a severe financial difficulty. Unlike my father, who saw fit to hold tight to his purse strings despite his son's troubles, Sir Prescott has been more than generous in helping me regain both my financial and social standing with the ton. I am greatly indebted both to him and to his cousin, Lady Geary, for their assistance."

She suppressed a knowing smile at the reference to Barbara. No longer quite such the naive country girl, she could easily guess how he had sought to repay Barbara for her assistance.

William took both their sherry glasses and set them on the low cherry wood table in front of them. He slid closer to her on the settee and her eyes flew to his. He gazed at her intently as he raised one of his large hands to stroke her hair. She felt his fingers trace the side of her face and then move across her lips. She had to bite back a gasp of surprise.

"Miss Royce, I realize you have not much experience

with these things, but I encourage you to consider how fortunate you are that Sir Prescott has deigned to make you his wife. I can assure you that he is a man of noble character. He has a considerate and generous spirit. You are most lucky that he has sought to make a match with you."

"Yes," Charlotte breathed, chewing on her full bottom lip in confusion as she felt rather than saw William's hand trace a line down from her face along the length of her neck to move across the tops of her breasts where they rose in large mounds above the plunging décolletage of her dinner gown.

His eyes had darkened to midnight and he continued speaking. "You do realize how fortunate you are to have Sir Prescott as your intended, do you not, Miss Royce?"

She nodded, unable to speak, as his hand moved lower and cupped her full breast, his hand large enough to enclose its generous swell. Instantly, she felt her nipple harden against his palm. He was no longer looking into her face as he spoke. His gaze had slid lower and was focused on where his hand moved on her body. His thumb brushed the erect nipple and she was unable to restrain a cry when he seized it between his thumb and forefinger and squeezed.

"Sir, you mustn't!"

She tried to pull away, but the edge of her skirt was trapped under the weight of his thigh and she found his other arm had come around her bare shoulders and was pulling her towards him.

The next thing she knew, she found herself seated across his lap, her hands trapped in one of his on her lap as he pressed kisses across the mounding swells of her breasts and continued to touch her throbbing nipples with his other hand. Her heart beat frantically and she felt incapable of drawing in enough air. With each panting gasp, she felt her breasts push more firmly into his embrace, her nipples thrusting against his fingers.

"Mr. Hathaway, I beg of you. This is most improper!"

He lifted his head to pin her with his searing gaze. "Miss Royce, I do not wish to be insulting, but you are obviously of the country and unknowledgeable of behavior considered acceptable within Society. I have told you that I hold your fiancé in the utmost respect, which I do."

He smoothed back a strand of her long blond hair that had become disheveled when she had tried to escape him.

"You must believe me when I say that I will do nothing to jeopardize my friendship with your fiancé. I have only his best interest at heart."

She couldn't help but stare at him in incredulity. How could his making love to her be in Sir Prescott's best interest?

A knock sounded at the drawing room door and interrupted whatever it was that William was about to say. Smoothly, as though nothing out of the ordinary had happened, he placed his hands around her waist and helped her rise. The intimate feel of his big hands enclosing her waist seemed almost more shocking than what he had just done. He kept one arm proprietarily about her waist as he led her across the room.

"Dinner is served," Hornby announced from the doorway.

They followed Hornby's portly figure across the hall to the dining room. For an instant, Charlotte entertained the idea of pleading a headache and escaping to the safety of her room, but the feel of William's hard hand at her waist spread a melting weakness through her bones. A small part of her brain reasoned that sitting across a dinner table from the man seemed a safe enough occupation. There would be servants in attendance, and she could always plead a headache later.

As the servants helped them take their seats, William dashed one of her hopes.

"As it is just Miss Royce and I for dinner, you do not need to remain. We will ring the bell when we have need of your assistance," he said.

Charlotte found herself seated at a table intimately set for two, their first course already in front of them.

"Claret, Miss Royce?" William held the decanter for her.

She looked suspiciously at the bottle and then up at him, remembering the last time he succeeded in making her drunk. As far as she could tell, there was no malicious intent in his eyes and she realized that refusing the wine would make her seem prudish, rude, and worse, as though she didn't trust him.

"Yes, I will have one glass, Mr. Hathaway," she said, emphasizing the number.

His lips curled into a laconic grin. "To Sir Prescott." He held his glass up to hers in a toast. "May you make him an excellent wife."

With the clink of their glasses, she wanted to ask him to explain how his earlier actions constituted respect for Sir Prescott's relationship with herself, but to do so would mean discussing what had happened earlier. Even thinking about his hands and lips on her caused her mouth to go dry and her knees to feel weak, so she said nothing.

Surprisingly, William behaved the perfect gentleman over dinner, regaling her with adventurous tales of his boyhood growing up with Simon in the south of England. It was obvious that though Simon stood to inherit the family fortune, he loved his brother and was not bitter about their very different destinies. As he spoke, she began to feel a growing curiosity about Simon.

"Your brother sounds like a wonderful man, Mr. Hathaway," she said as she finished the final course.

"You are lucky, Miss Royce, as you will have the opportunity to meet him next week."

"Indeed?"

"Yes, he is one of the guests attending the festivities Sir Prescott has arranged."

"I hope, Mr. Hathaway, that you will do me the honors

of an introduction."

"But of course. Now," he said rising to his feet and coming around the table to assist her, "Let us retire once more to the drawing room for an after dinner drink."

Now was her chance to make her getaway, she realized, and yet she found herself saying nothing. William's stories of Simon and the obvious love he felt for his brother had made him seem less frightening. Indeed, to her surprise, she found herself thinking William to be a rather likable man.

With her thoughts so directed, she didn't notice when William dismissed the staff for the night and neither did she hear the click of the lock as he sealed the drawing room door. He escorted her to the settee by the fire.

"Another sherry, Miss Royce, or perhaps you, too, would like a glass of port?" He walked to the bar on the sideboard.

"No thank-you, Mr. Hathaway." She gazed into the flames of the fire. The night had grown cool and the fire's radiant heat felt good against her bare arms and face.

When William returned to the settee, to her surprise, he did not sit down. Instead, he placed his glass of port on the low cherry wood table and knelt at her feet.

"Now, where were we?" he said as though speaking to himself. He placed his hands on her ankles.

"Mr. Hathaway?" she looked down at him in surprise. "What are you doing?"

"I am doing my good friend a favor," he said, his hands traveling up her legs and pushing back her skirts.

"What?" she gasped, feeling his lips on the side of her knee.

She tried to wiggle away from him, but his large hands caught her upper thighs through the fine material of her gown, spreading them wide and holding them firmly open. He raised his head to pin her with his sharp gaze.

"Isn't it obvious, Miss Royce?" he said, pushing her skirts to her waist, his lips now tracing the sensitive skin of her inner thigh.

"Obvious?" she gasped, trying to keep track of the conversation, but she could swear she felt his tongue moistening her heated flesh.

She clenched the velvet seat cushions and fought to keep from moaning when his mouth came perilously close to the juncture between her thighs. William rose so he could look her in the face, positioning his long lean body between her legs, his muscular chest pressed against the soft pillow of her breasts. His big hand was hard and warm and it cupped her hot core through her petticoats.

"You have admitted, Miss Royce, that you are a young genteel woman of the country, unschooled in the ways of Society."

She writhed against him as she felt his hand move the petticoats aside to touch her moist heat and begin to rub against her, the action causing jolting shocks of awareness to rip through her body. Her nipples instantly hardened against the thin material of her bodice and she couldn't help but savor their aching peaks pressing against his warm chest.

"Unlike you, your fiancé is a mature man of vast experience and refined tastes." As he spoke, William' hand rubbed relentlessly against her throbbing center.

She tried to close her legs and escape his merciless hand but that simply brought her bare thighs in contact with the velvet of his trousers and the firm body underneath. She could no longer bite back the soft moan that escaped her parted lips. His other hand came up to caress her jutting breast through the bodice of her gown. She cried out helplessly as he squeezed the nipple while simultaneously touching her intimately beneath her skirts. She felt a rich moisture coat his hand as he rubbed.

"Over the years, he has cultivated a particular aesthetic with regard to his taste in women. It is no secret, Miss Royce, that he prefers women of a certain experience and sensibility."

Charlotte wasn't sure how much more she could stand. The sensations building in her body were much like those Sir Prescott had engendered when he had kissed her breasts, but the feel of William's hand against her moist core transported her completely beyond that earlier level of awareness and longing. She writhed, pinned and helpless under his big frame.

"Like all gentlemen with healthy appetites, your fiancé has kept mistresses for years."

"Mistresses?" She panted, her breath coming in short pants.

"Remember, Miss Royce, your fiancé is a man of the world. I do not wish to shock you, but within Society, gentlemen most often maintain mistresses, especially an unmarried man such as your Sir Prescott has been."

Just when she felt like her body would explode, like she was on the verge of a momentous experience, William removed his hands from her and pushed back into a sitting position beside her on the settee. Her eyes flew to his, startled at his sudden departure, and she realized with embarrassment that her body was sprawled wantonly against the settee, her breasts rising and falling rapidly against her bodice, her skirts rucked about her waist, a warm moisture seeping between her legs.

She stared dazedly up at William, for a moment unable to do anything but lie there and absurdly wish he would resume his attentions to her body. Instead, his gaze traveled over her, his eyes glinting as they took in the flush of her bosom above the décolletage, her parted lips and shining eyes, the secret pink skin, moist beneath her skirts and now exposed to his view.

"It is no secret amongst Sir Prescott's friends what kind of woman he desires, Miss Royce, as his mistresses have all been of a most distinctive type. I wish not to cause you shock or dismay, but you are not of the same caliber."

His words made her feel chilled as the cool air brushed over her bare flesh. She made to sit up and straighten out the skirt of her gown, but William quickly seized her hands in his, preventing her from doing so and positioning his body once more between her thighs.

"Remain as you are, Miss Royce," he commanded, his voice husky and deep.

With his big hands holding hers captive, she knew she was at his mercy.

"Are you going to ravish me now?" she couldn't help asking in small voice.

He laughed, and the vibrations caused her nipples to erect again against the solid wall of his chest.

"Miss Royce, your innocence is refreshing."

His lips closed on one of her nipples through the thin material of her bodice and she gasped as she felt him tug at it with his teeth. She struggled futilely under his massive weight, suddenly becoming aware of his protuberance through the velvet of his trousers pressing intimately against her thigh. She struggled harder.

He raised his head to look down at her flushed face and she gasped as he placed his hand once more on the junction of her thighs.

"I will not dishonor my friend by compromising his fiancé, Miss Royce. Your virginity is safe with me."

With those words, William pressed a long finger against her core. She gasped as she felt him move his finger slowly forward and into her.

"Heavens, Sir, what are you doing?" she cried.

As his finger slowly sunk into her tight depths, his thumb moved over a wildly sensitive part of her. His other hand slid her gown from her shoulders and down to her waist, exposing her bosom to his view. He began to caress her heaving breast, cupping and molding the shape, his thumb and forefinger tormenting her throbbing nipple. His mouth tasted the tender flesh beneath her ear.

"I am preparing you for your fiancé, Miss Royce. You do want to please him, to make him satisfied in his marriage to you, I am sure. Consider this your education."

Another finger joined the one moving inside her, and then he slowly slid both out and then back in. A slow rhythm grew, his tongue in her ear, his hand on her breast, his fingers moving in and out of her tight, moist passage.

"Please, stop," she whimpered, the feelings overwhelming.

"Your education, Miss Royce," his voice was a low growl in her ear.

The heavy, uneven cadence of his breathing combined with the other sensations coursing through her body, a crescendo of feeling overloading her control, causing something to suddenly snap within her.

"Sir!" she gasped.

A million pulsating nerve endings seemed to explode all at once. She felt a gush of moisture release from her body and wet his hand as he withdrew his fingers from inside her snug sheath. She looked up into his face, dazed. High color marked the skin at his neck and across his cheeks. His white, even teeth were clenched and the strong lines of his jaw stood out in sharp relief. He eased away from her and reclaimed his glass of port.

"Congratulations, Miss Royce. You have just had your first lesson in womanhood."

She could see that his hand was shaking slightly as he brought the crystal to his lips. After a long draught, he set it back on the table. He observed her as she lay wantonly against the settee. The intensity of what she had experienced had drained her and left her with little energy to right her dress. As it was, her breasts were bare and her gown was still hiked about her waist, exposing her femininity to his heated gaze.

"You have begun to learn how to receive pleasure. Now, you must learn the first lesson in how to give pleasure to a man."

She watched in helpless fascination as his hands came to the front of his trousers and began unbuttoning them. He rose to his feet beside the settee and now at her eye level she could see his red baton bare in front of her. Unlike Hornby the butler, whose baton had barely been able to protrude beyond the enormous bulk of his gut, William's flesh stood long and large, jutting upwards proudly from the front of his black velvet trousers.

He studied her intently as she looked upon his flesh. His breathing had altered slightly, coming quickly and unevenly. She watched as one of his hands gripped himself.

"This, Miss Royce, is my penis."

His hand momentarily stroked the hard flesh and she saw his hips thrust forward slightly, involuntarily. He bit back a small groan. He moved closer to her, his hand still holding himself.

"Touch me," he said on an exhale, removing his hand from his turgid flesh.

She saw the intensity in William's gaze, the high color staining his cheeks, and she heard his altered breathing. For a moment, she was afraid of him as he loomed over her, his flesh bare to her gaze, and she contemplated a means of escape. But then she remembered Sir Prescott's reaction when she touched him.

She suddenly realized that all three men, Hornby, Sir Prescott and William, experienced pleasure by touching or by being touched on their penises. To her surprise, she felt a sense of power replace her fear. She knew instinctively that if she reached out and touched William as he commanded she would give him pleasure. If she refused, he would suffer.

"Touch me," William repeated, thrusting his hips forward so that his flesh was almost in her face.

She studied him for one last moment, recalling the pleasure he had given her. She admired how beautiful he was and that he wanted her to do something for him. A slight smile touched her lips and she lifted her hand to enclose his rigid flesh.

"Like this?" she asked, repeating the motions that Sir

Prescott had shown her.

His flesh was almost hot to the touch, ribbed with veins, and yet the skin itself was silky smooth. She noticed how small and white her hand looked wrapped around him. With her hand encircling him, she realized how much thicker and longer he was than Sir Prescott. His flesh pulsed rhythmically like a heartbeat.

"Yes." The word was a sibilant hiss coming from William's clenched teeth. His face was contorted almost as if he were in pain.

"Am I doing this correctly?" she asked, concerned she was hurting him. She stopped the rhythmic movement of her hand sliding up and down the length of him and relaxed her grip.

William jerked her hand away from him.

"Enough!" he said. "I see you have already been acquainted with this activity, so let us proceed to the next."

He grasped her shoulders and turned her body on the settee to face him as he stood in front of her.

"Take me in your mouth." Holding his flesh in his large hand, he presented himself to her.

"Sir?" Her blue eyes flew to his, shocked at the request.

It was one thing to touch him with her hand; it would be quite another to put her mouth on him. He didn't answer her question. Instead, he clamped his other hand on the back of her head, wrapping his fingers in her hair. The next thing she knew, his penis pressed against her lower lip. Still looking up into his face, she saw his pupils dilate almost black on contact with her mouth.

"Kiss me," he grunted.

She was caught within his embrace, his one hand on the back of her head, forcing her forward, and the other guiding his hard flesh to her mouth. With his movement toward her, she felt her bare breasts brush the velvet encasing his thighs, the sensation exquisite and distracting, and she realized the intimacy of her position with his big body surrounding her. Clenching the seat cushions of the settee with both hands, she pursed her lips and placed a kiss on the tip of his long, heated flesh. When she tried to pull back so she could look up at him again, his hand against the back of her head pushed her firmly back.

"Open your mouth," he said, his hand momentarily stroking his turgid length.

She wanted to ask him why, but the instant she opened her mouth to speak, she found him inside her, her lips spread wide to accommodate his engorged flesh.

"Yes, but no teeth!" he growled, pushing further into her mouth. "Now, suck."

His flesh was warm, textured, and tasted slightly salty. She felt him touch the back of her throat and she almost gagged. She reached to push against his thighs to try and create some space between them. His hands instantly clamped each of hers and stilled her movement. With her head no longer held captive, she twisted it to the side, freeing her mouth of his penis.

"Mr. Hathaway, I can't breathe!" she exclaimed.

"My apologies, Miss Royce." His voice sounded rueful, and when she looked up into his face, she saw that his expression was one of wry self-mockery. "You are doing very well with this lesson and giving me a great deal of pleasure. I must admit that I became a little overenthusiastic." One of his hands kept hers captive, the other came out to cup her bare breast and then tease the nipple.

"Mr. Hathaway?"

"You are an apt pupil, Miss Royce. There is one last lesson for tonight. I will release your hands if you promise to do exactly as I tell you. Do you understand?"

Charlotte nodded, worrying her full lower lip between her teeth as she looked up at him and wondered what that lesson might be.

"Good, now use your hands like this." He took her hands and wrapped them around his heated length. "Place me within your mouth again."

She tentatively opened her mouth, and again found her lips pushed wide to encompass his large member.

"Good," he said, exhaling, his hands coming up to caress and torment her breasts as his hips began to slowly thrust forward and back. "Very good, Miss Royce."

It sounded as though his words were spoken through clenched teeth, but Charlotte had her face full of him, his penis moving back and forth in her mouth as she sucked and her hands stroking the length of him. His hands on her breasts began to affect her and she felt moisture pool between her thighs. She held back the small moan forming at the back of her throat as his penis slurped in and out of her mouth. The tempo increased and she heard him groan. Just when she thought her jaw would crack from the force of him moving against her, he suddenly withdrew. He pointed his penis at her breasts and she watched as what seemed like a large quantity of white fluid squirt from the end of his flesh and across the swelling mounds of her breasts.

"Oh yes," he sighed. "Very good."

His hand pumped his flesh and a few more droplets anointed the tops of her breasts.

The warm liquid quickly cooled against her bosom and it had a distinctive, unique scent. She tried to think of a corollary but could think of nothing. She looked up at him and noticed that his face had lost some of its hardness. Indeed, it seemed to her as if it had softened. The heightened color was fading.

In a deft series of movements, he rebuttoned his breeches. Standing before her, he looked remarkably as if nothing had transpired. For a long moment, he gazed down at her, his eyes moving from her bared breasts, her nipples still erect from his ministrations, to the pink flesh and white legs exposed by her skirts still rucked about her waist. A white smile lit his dark face as he leaned over her.

"Allow me, Miss Royce," he said, pulling a kerchief from his coat pocket and wiping the sticky fluid from her bosom.

He then sat beside her on the settee and quickly pulled her skirts down over her legs. Before refastening the bodice of her gown, he placed a long lingering kiss on each of her breasts, and Charlotte was unable to bite back the gasp of surprise as she felt her body heat once more with desire.

"It has been a pleasure to educate you, Miss Royce, in the ways of the flesh."

He rose to his feet and held out a hand to her, bringing her to her feet.

"It is growing rather late, so let me bid you goodnight. Upon the morrow, I look forward to your further instruction."

He escorted her without incident to the door of her bedroom, and without so much as a kiss goodnight, disappeared down the hall to his rooms.

*****

4 CHARLOTTE MEETS THE EARL OF RADWAY

The next morning, Charlotte could not accept what had happened the night before. The memories of how William had touched her and of how he had made her touch him caused a slow burn to move through her body, making it ache in unfamiliar and peculiar ways. She couldn't help worrying about Sir Prescott and wondering if she had betrayed him.

She also remembered that the Gearys were to return that coming evening and the idea of facing them after what William had done made her face flush with embarrassment. He had told her he would continue her lessons today and the unsettling idea reminded her of how she had seen him dally with Barbara the first day of her arrival at Wharton Manse. Would he so casually go from intimacies with her to then renewed intimacies with Barbara? The thought was most distressing and unacceptable to her. But he was a rake, she told herself. That was how rakes behaved. But then she also remembered how he had acted gentlemanly and considerate with her and how he had given her so much earth-shattering pleasure.

As she rose from bed, she knew she could not in good conscience face William alone again. She would hide in her rooms until the Gearys returned. She rang Alice and requested a tray be brought to her room for breakfast.

"Ye be not feeling well, Miss?" Alice asked when she came in.

"I am just tired, Alice, but thank-you for asking. I think I will rest in my rooms until the Gearys arrive this evening."

"Will ye be having dinner with them?"

"Yes, but until then, I will rest."

***

Exhausted by the emotional and physical upheaval of the night before, Charlotte fell into a heavy slumber after breakfast. She began to dream. First she was at Quigley Hall. Her whole family was there, including her father, and they were all happy together. Then, she found herself in a dark garden at night. A tall man loomed beside her. She trusted the man, knowing instinctively that he would do nothing to hurt her, and in the dream, she yearned for him, wanting him to touch her. She felt his hands begin to touch her breasts, rubbing and caressing them, causing exquisite sensations to shimmer through her body. In the dream, she was free to move. She wore no clothes and the man's hands traveled freely over her as she writhed in pleasure. The garden was dark and she couldn't make out the features of the man. Was it Sir Prescott? William? He was dark, tall, and big, but the garden was black as night and she could not see his face.

Suddenly, she found herself on her hands and knees, still in the dark garden, and felt the cool grass under her hands. She felt rather than saw his large warm body wrap around hers. The man's thighs spread her legs apart. His lips whispered into her ear, the words indistinct. She could feel a big hand on her breast, cupping and teasing it to a peaked awareness. Then, she felt the hands firm on her hips, moving her back against something blunt, warm, and hard. A pressure began to build against her core as the thing pushed into her. Then, the pressure eased. Back and forth, again and again, the pressure would build, and then stop. She felt moisture seep down against her thighs and she wanted to scream in erotic frustration, wanting something to happen but she knew not what.

"Yes, let it happen." A voice in her ear caused her to awake with a start and sit bolt upright in bed.

"Mr. Hathaway!" William was reclining beside her on the bed, his body had been wrapped around hers. To her shock, his hand was under her nightgown, buried between her thighs, his fingers stroking the moisture pooling there.

She wriggled away from him, shielding herself by pulling a pillow against her body.

"What are you doing in my room?" she asked breathlessly, tossing her hair back from her overheated face and trying to wake up from the dream that still made her thighs quiver and her breasts erect where they pressed into the pillow.

"Isn't that obvious, Miss Royce. I am continuing your education."

He smiled, bringing his hand to his mouth and wrapped his sensual lips around the fingers he had been intimately stroking her with. Her brows rose in shocked amazement as he sucked and then licked his fingers.

"You taste good, Miss Royce. I hope you found me as tasty last night," he grinned.

She felt a blush spread up her neck and across her cheeks at the memory.

"But how did you get in here?" She looked toward the door.

"As anyone would, Miss Royce, I opened the door."

She frowned, mentally kicking herself. She had forgotten to lock the door after Alice had removed the breakfast tray.

"Don't worry, Miss Royce. The door is locked now, so we will not be interrupted, and the servants have been instructed not to disturb me. They think I am ensconced in the study working on one of Sir Prescott's projects. We are free to continue with your education."

"Mr. Hathaway." Charlotte chose her words carefully. "You have been most considerate to concern yourself with my, um, education." She felt the blush heat her face again, remembering the feel of his hands, his fingers probing within her. "But, you do not need to continue to concern yourself with me. I assure you, I now feel quite prepared to face my duties as Sir Prescott's intended, so you see, you don't need to worry about me. Besides, the Gearys return this evening and I'm sure Barbara will need you."

She bit her lower lip as the last words slipped out, and her eyes flew to William, wondering what he would do now that he new she was aware of his relationship with Barbara. He laughed, and she noted with dismay how dashingly attractive he looked. He had discarded his waistcoat and cravat on the chair by the bed and his white linen shirt hung open to the middle of his chest. His black hair had come free of its tie, his dark locks falling to his shoulders. His long legs were encased in skintight tan breeches. She could well imagine Barbara's attraction to the man. He was everything a woman could wish for, she admitted with chagrin.

"Miss Royce, please do not concern yourself with Lady Geary. I assure you, what transpires between the two of us has no bearing on your future relation."

When she made to protest, William continued, pulling the pillow roughly from her, his eyes raking her thin nightgown and the shape of her breasts outlined beneath.

"But don't worry, Miss Royce. I understand you are concerned about the timing. I will make sure that we end this lesson well before you will be required to dress for dinner."

Before she could object, she found herself pushed back into the pillows, her thighs forced wide open as William pressed his big body hard against hers, his hands sliding her nightgown up about her waist. One of his hands clasped both of her hands together and pushed her arms above her head, which caused her body to arch upwards and into his heated length.

"Mr. Hathaway!" she gasped, trying to object but finding his hand clamped to her mouth.

"You have nothing to fear, Miss Royce. Let me remind you, as I have said previously, I only have your best intentions in mind."

Releasing her hands, he braced himself above her on one elbow, using his free hand to untie the laces of her nightgown, pushing it down to free her breasts.

"I assure you, Miss Royce, your education is not yet complete," he said against the side of her breast before he slid her erect nipple into his mouth.

Her arms came up to push him off her, but he was too heavy, an immovable force pushing her into the soft mattress. She couldn't stop her hands from lightly stroking across his hard back, feeling the contours of the solid planes and the resilient muscle. She felt his tongue stroke her, his mouth opening wide to suck in a large portion of her breast, and she was unable to stop the moan that gathered in the back of her throat at the wild sensations he generated in her body. Her bare legs moved against the tight material of his breeches and she felt him pressing hard and hot against her inner thigh. Her dream suddenly returned to her, memories of the mysterious man wrapped about her, and she realized that she wanted William inside of her. She wiggled her behind, maneuvering his prodding flesh against her entrance, feeling the rough cloth of his breeches rub against her sensitized, moist flesh. She wrapped her arms around his waist, pulling him closer and felt his flesh subtly pulse where it pressed against her. Her thighs quivered in yearning.

"Easy, Miss Royce." William lifted his head to gaze down into her face. "You seek to graduate before you have learned this particular lesson."

He studied her heated face, noting her ragged breathing and dilated pupils. His eyes traveled lower, taking in her breasts, rigid and flushed where his mouth had touched her. She tugged at her bottom lip with her teeth, unable to do anything but stare up at him and feel the throbbing pulse of his flesh against her moist core.

"Good, I see that you are ready, Miss Royce," he said, easing himself down between her thighs.

Startled, she watched his head move lower. She felt his lips whisper light kisses along her stomach, his hands pushing her knees wider open and then caressing the sensitive flesh of her inner thighs.

"Mr. Hathaway!" she breathed. "What are you doing?"

He did not respond, but moved his head even lower. Her hands clenched the sheets convulsively as she felt his mouth touch her moist core.

"My heavens!" she exclaimed, both shocked and appalled to consider what he was doing. But then all thoughts of propriety were swept away as she felt his lips, tongue and mouth begin to move fluidly against her, tasting, touching, teasing her sensitive flesh. Her hands left the sheets to rifle through his dark hair. She felt a pressure repeatedly enter her and then retreat. Was it his fingers? His tongue? She realized it felt not quite enough, but then he returned his attention to the juncture of her thighs, that secret place of hers that caused wildfire to course through her blood. She lay back and submitted herself to his masterful manipulation of her body. He played her like a finely crafted instrument, and the pressure built in intensity within her. She gasped for air and for something else, some kind of release from the sensual torment.

"Sing for me, Miss Royce."

She felt his breath warm against the inside of her thigh.

"Please, please," she begged, the intensity building to a violent storm, and suddenly, when she thought she could stand no more, her body convulsed wildly and she was unable to bite back the scream that escaped her trembling lips.

"Yes!"

Her eyes fluttered closed and her body fell back limply against the sheets.

When she could finally open her eyes again, she saw William sitting beside her on the bed, a slight smile touching his lips. He reached out to caress the side of her face, his thumb tracing her full lower lip.

"Very good, Miss Royce. Very good." His voice was low and husky, the color high on his cheeks.

Suddenly, a knock sounded on the door.

"Miss Charlotte, you be awake?" The doorknob rattled and Alice's voice sounded from the hallway.

Her eyes flew to William. He held a finger against his lips and then quickly and quietly retrieved his cravat and waistcoat from the chair. He picked up his boots in the other hand and walked silently to the private sitting room adjoining the bedroom. There was another door into the hallway from there from which William could make his escape. She hurried to straighten her nightgown and her hair before answering the door.

"Just a minute," she called and then opened the door.

The maid's eyes widened when she noted Charlotte's flushed cheeks and dilated eyes, but she didn't immediately comment.

"The Gearys and Miss Fetzer have returned, Miss. They be hoping to see ye for tea. Would you care to join them?" Alice's manner was formal, restrained.

"Yes, of course," she nodded.

She quickly selected a dress to wear. As Alice helped her into it in front of the full length mirror, Charlotte noticed how stiffly the maid was behaving.

"Is something bothering you?" she asked.

"If ye must know, Miss, I am concerned about you and Mr. Hathaway."

Charlotte's eyes widened, surprised at the audacity of the maid to question the nature of her relationships.

"Excuse me?" she said, turning to face Alice, who had the decency to duck her head when she replied.

"I know it not be me place to say nothing, Miss, but Mr. Hathaway be paying you too much attention. Sir Prescott is a good and fine master and I not be wanting ye to play him for a fool."

This was too much. Charlotte frowned at her maid.

"How dare you question my loyalty to my fiancé! And to accuse me of carrying on with Mr. Hathaway is unbelievable."

She realized that if she wasn't careful, she would sound too defensive, so she changed her tactic.

"Let me remind you of something, Alice. You made it clear to me that your relationship with Hornby was a private matter between the two of you. Remember?"

The maid nodded her head, sullenly.

"Well, I would request that you grant me the same courtesy, and respect the privacy of my relationship with Sir Prescott. Let assure you, though I go beyond the call of duty to do so, that I have done nothing, nor will I do anything, to compromise my commitment to your Master. Do you understand?"

Alice looked up for a moment, her brown eyes studying Charlotte, and then she nodded, this time with an air of acceptance.

"Yes, Miss. I understand."

***

The number of people in the parlor startled Charlotte. She had no time to compose herself, because as soon as she entered the room, they all turned to look at her.

Barbara emerged from the group and came forward to take her hand, her sherry-colored eyes studying Charlotte's face for a moment and then traveling quickly over her body, taking in the beautiful day dress. She appeared satisfied, because she gave Charlotte a quick smile and squeeze of the hand before turning to face the group.

"Everyone, please allow me the pleasure of introducing to you Miss Charlotte Royce, the fiancé of our gracious host, my cousin Edmund Prescott, Earl of Wharton."

Charlotte had vowed to herself that the next time she encountered Barbara and Sally she would not act the naive country girl, but with so many eyes on her, she couldn't help the blush that spread up and across her bosom revealed by the moderate cut of her bodice and flushed her cheeks.

Barbara escorted her past Sir Geary to an older couple seated near the tea table.

"Charlotte, these are Edmund and my old family friends, the Horns."

Charlotte curtsied, abruptly realizing when she looked at Caroline Horn that the woman was close in age to Sir Prescott. As Barbara led her to the next introduction, Charlotte had the disturbing thought that if Caroline looked old enough to be her grandmother then Sir Prescott was old enough to be her grandfather.

"And this is John and Sabrina Singer. John is Edmund's nephew on his sister's side."

The young couple was obviously in love. John held Sabrina's hand and Charlotte had to fight the urge not to stare at Sabrina's protruding stomach. It was obvious the young woman was very much pregnant.

A swift image of herself pregnant swept through her mind, but before she could think about the implications of having Sir Prescott's child, Barbara led her to the next group of people. The piercing gaze of the man Barbara approached took her breath away. She instantly dropped her eyes from his, fighting the blush she knew was threatening to stain her cheeks.

The man stood beside William and another man. Sally was also among the group. With the man's intense gaze pinning her, Charlotte was oblivious to everyone else in the group. Even William's handsome presence and the memories of their intimate time together earlier in the day failed to unsettle her as much as the feel of this man's eyes on her.

"You know my dear friend, Sally Fetzer, and Mr. Hathaway, of course," Barbara said. "But please let me introduce you to Mr. Hathaway's brother, Sir Lowell, the new Earl of Radway."

Charlotte dared to raise her eyes briefly to the man, curious to see the brother William had described to her. Noting that like his brother William he was tall and lean, Charlotte thought he might perhaps be slightly shorter and more muscular. His face too was chiseled with classic features, but his features were harder, more severe, and a small scar marred the line of one dark brow.

Unlike William's pale skin and black hair, Simon's skin was darker, his long hair a tawny shade of brown and tied back in a queue. Despite his clothes being simple and of a less fashionable cut than his brother's, she could tell they were of the finest quality. He eschewed the fancy cravats the other men wore for a simple, snowy white swath of cloth at his neck. Where his brother exuded a rakish masculine sensuality, Simon struck her as more untamed, a more ruthless breed of male. He seemed infinitely more dangerous to her. Still, after all his brother had said of him, she couldn't think of him as Sir Lowell but simply as Simon, the older brother William respected and loved. In the fleeting moment her eyes met his, she saw that instead of blue they glowed an intriguing shade of hazel, perhaps more green than brown.

As she dipped a curtsy for the gentleman, she realized that if Simon was now Earl of Radway then it must mean that his father and William's had died. Her eyes flew back up to his and then briefly to William, who was watching their introduction with a slight smile playing tilting his sensual lips.

"I am sorry to hear of your father's passing," she said, before realizing that her words revealed an improper, overly intimate knowledge of his family's affairs.

A tense silence followed her words and she immediately wished she could retract them. Not knowing where to look, she kept her eyes focused on the top button of his black coat directly beneath the snowy white neck cloth. She was unaware of the glances that passed between the other members of the group.

Finally, he spoke, his voice deeper than his brother's and it had a rough quality that caused frissons of awareness through her body.

"Thank-you for your condolences, Miss Royce."

When she risked another glance upward, she was surprised to see the anger in his eyes as his gaze met hers and then swept insolently down her body.

"My brother speaks highly of you, Miss Royce."

He looked pointedly at William and Charlotte was confused by the anger she felt emanating from him toward his brother.

"And this is Mr. Bollinger, one of Mr. Hathaway's friends and an expert hunter."

Barbara's words broke the uneasy tension Charlotte could feel building between the two brothers. She vaguely registered the third man, who was stockier than both Simon and William, with a head of curly blond hair.

Because her attention was focused almost exclusively on Simon and how he glared at his brother, she did not notice the predatory gleam that entered Bollinger's eyes as he watched her drop a curtsy in front of him, his eyes traveling to her cleavage that was more clearly exposed to him as she bent toward him.

"My pleasure, Miss Royce," he said.

Startling her from her thoughts of Simon, Mr. Bollinger

took her hand and pressed a moist kiss to the back of it. For the first time, she took notice of the man and shuddered at the feel of his lips on her. She had to fight the urge to wipe her hand against her skirt when he released her. She saw his colorless blue eyes, beady in his round, flushed face, staring at her. There was something about the man that made her distinctly uncomfortable.

"Thank-you for the introductions, Barbara. I think I will have some tea." Charlotte excused herself hastily from the group, wanting to escape the scrutiny of so many people studying her, assessing her, judging her.

As she walked to the tea table, myriad sensations coursed through her. She was used to quiet living among intimate friends, not to this public exposure with so many eyes of people she did not know trained upon her. She forced herself to stand tall, squaring her shoulders, as she headed for the tea table, and she forced herself to ignore the prickle of awareness at the back of her neck that told her Simon was watching her. Unfortunately, when she turned back to the room having poured her cup of tea she noted that Mr. Bollinger was also watching her.

She pointedly ignored their eyes. Instead, sipping her tea, she studied the dynamics of the various parties in the room. The Singers were speaking with the Horns and Mr. Geary. Sally was shamelessly hanging against Simon, the action thrusting her small pert breast against his arm. She was gazing up into his face as he spoke with a look of adoration. As far as Charlotte could tell, he seemed oblivious to Sally's flirtations as he spoke with William and Mr. Bollinger. Barbara was subtler than Sally, though knowing what she did, Charlotte could see the intimacy that existed between Barbara and William when she lightly touched his knee to emphasize a point.

She decided that it would be safest if she joined the other group, so she sat down next to Caroline Horn and listened to Sir Geary and Mr. Horn regale the Singers about their travels on the Continent.

***

Dinner that evening did not go as Charlotte had thought it would. As Alice had helped her dress in the sumptuous burgundy dinner gown with its plunging bodice and pin her hair up above her head in a golden crown of braids, she had worried about having to endure Simon's piercing stare and his peculiar disapproval of her. At the same time, however, she had perversely wanted to be the most attractive woman in the room and she had paid particular care with her dress. But her concerns were unfounded.

She found herself seated at the opposite end from him at the formal dinner table, which was set for ten. She was placed next to Mr. Horn, who occupied one end of the table. Caroline Horn sat across from her, and to her dismay, she found Mr. Bollinger sitting directly beside her.

Mr. Horn was a talker, and over the long course of the dinner as he waxed merry about everything from his wife and his travels in the south of France to the current price of wool, Mr. Bollinger whispered in Charlotte's ear.

At first, he whispered about the food. "Would you like more of the cream sauce?"

His hand brushed hers in a blatant manner when he passed her the tureen. The feel of his hot, moist breath against her ear caused a shiver of repulsion to course through her. There was something about the man she found repelling. She remembered the first dinner she had had with William, when he had begun his flirtation with her. She had been embarrassed and disturbed by his attentions, but not disgusted.

When Mr. Bollinger began to whisper more intimate things in her ear, like how he wanted to dance with her, hold her, touch her, it was all Charlotte could do to keep from leaping to her feet and running away from him. Her efforts to silence him, her frigid frowns of disapproval and then her attempts to tell him to stop had no effect. She was also aware that William, who sat next to Caroline, was watching the interaction, an amused expression on his face. She did not want to give him any satisfaction by revealing her discomfiture, so she bit her bottom lip and tried to ignore the increasingly lurid comments Mr. Bollinger whispered into her ear.

At long last, the final course was finished, and Charlotte drew a breath of relief at being able to escape Mr. Bollinger's attentions. Everyone rose to retire to the drawing room and the ladies moved into the parlor for their sherries while the men partook of port and cigars.

"Warwick Manse seems to agree with you," Sally said to Charlotte, pouring her a sherry. She watched her closely.

Barbara joined them and also watched her. No longer quite so naive, Charlotte had prepared herself for this interview, knowing that at least Barbara had a vested interest in how William and she had gotten along while the Gearys were away.

"Yes, I am growing accustomed to life here," she said, congratulating herself on the cool manner in which she uttered the words.

"I trust Mr. Hathaway was attentive during our absence?" Barbara asked, training her sherry-colored eyes on Charlotte.

Mr. Hathaway was the perfect gentleman," Charlotte said smoothly, again happy to find herself speaking coolly and without any hint of naive or excessive emotion. No blush fired her cheeks. She had to admit that maybe it had been right of William to offer her an education in the affairs of the sexes. She now felt completely unruffled by the pointed queries of the other two women.

"Good, I am glad," Barbara said, apparently satisfied by her response. The jealousy that might have been there in her eyes was now gone. It was obvious that Barbara no longer viewed Charlotte a threat to her dalliance with William.

When the women rejoined the men in the drawing room, Mr. Singer insisted on playing the piano so that there might be some dancing. His wife being pregnant had retired early, and he felt it only right that Sally as an unattached woman should have the opportunity to dance as well. Unfortunately, in one of her unsuccessful efforts to stop Mr. Bollinger's unwanted attentions at the dinner table, Charlotte had agreed to dance with him.

As soon as Mr. Singer began to play, Charlotte found herself pulled into Mr. Bollinger's arms. Unlike the traditional country dances she was familiar with, this dance seemed highly improper, his one arm about her waist, his other clasping her hand in his at their shoulders.

"Mr. Bollinger, what kind of dance is this?" She couldn't help asking, though she knew it revealed her lack of cultural sophistication.

He grinned, his stubby teeth parted and his tongue appearing wet at the corner of his lips before he answered her. She fought the urge to turn away from him as he spoke.

"It's a waltz, my dear. It is all the rage in London, don't you know. Relax." His arm tightened against her waist, pulling her forcibly against his short, stout body.

She turned her head to the side, shuddering as she felt his eyes move across her cleavage where it was pressed tightly to his chest. As she looked about the room, she noticed Simon was dancing with Sally. Her eyes met his and held. To her dismay, she noticed his piercing gaze look assessingly at her and Mr. Bollinger. She couldn't help blushing, knowing he must see how Mr. Bollinger was manhandling her. She forced herself to look away from his angry stare. Mr. Bollinger was whispering in her ear again, his hand at her waist moving slightly, rubbing the smooth satin of her gown along her hip.

"Just follow my lead, my dear, and you will be fine." His hot, moist breath again came in her ear and she struggled against a rising tide of nausea.

Thankfully, the waltz finished, but then to her surprise, she found herself in William's arms as Mr. Singer started up the next tune. Unlike Mr. Bollinger, William didn't crowd her and the country-dance was one she knew. As William held her hand and spun her about, she couldn't help contrasting how different she felt in his arms than in Mr. Bollinger's. It wasn't just that he was much more attractive than Mr. Bollinger but that she felt comfortable in his presence. As he brought her close against him and she felt his eyes dip to her décolletage, she experienced none of the revulsion she had with Mr. Bollinger. She realized she had come to trust him.

"You are awfully quiet this evening, Miss Royce," he said. "Are you angry that we were interrupted with our lesson this afternoon?"

Her eyes flew to his and she saw that he was jesting. It was obvious that now that Barbara had returned he would no longer have time for her "education" as he called it. She decided to change the subject when the dance brought them close together again.

"Why is your brother angry with you?" Her question wiped the light mockery from William's expression.

"Simon can be such a stickler for convention sometimes," was all he said, a slight frown marring his perfect lips.

Charlotte declined Mr. Bollinger's request for the next dance. Instead, she sat with the Horns, sipping a cool drink and watching the other dancers move gracefully about the room, trying to ignore Mr. Bollinger's lurid stare. Barbara was in William's arms, obviously enraptured to be so close once more to her lover. Charlotte was surprised to find that she felt no jealousy toward the other woman. In that instant, she realized there was no way that she could love William. He was devilishly attractive and spectacularly appealing to look at, but she felt no emotional connection to him.

She felt oddly relieved at the realization, but then she

turned her gaze toward William's brother. Simon was dancing again with Sally, and like Barbara, Sally was overtly flirting with the man. But to her surprise, Charlotte felt a swift stab of jealously. She realized she wanted to be the one in his arms. She wanted to feel his hands on her. The thought was disturbing, and for a moment, she wondered how she would feel if Sir Prescott were there.

The music ended and she heard Barbara calling out, "One more waltz, please, John."

She also heard Sally's quieter voice speaking to Simon nearby. "You really should dance at least once with her, you know. It's only polite."

Before she could figure out to whom Sally was referring, she found Simon's tall form looming over her.

"May I have the honor of this dance, Miss Royce?"

She looked up into those distinctive hazel-green eyes, unable to do anything for a moment but stare, her own eyes wide, her mouth instantly dry. She swallowed, chewing for a moment on her full lower lip, but she found herself unable to speak, so instead she inclined her head.

And then she was in his arms, her gown swirling intimately against his long legs as they moved about the room. She studied the top button of his coat, still unable to find her voice. Instead, she reveled in the feel of his strong arms about her, his large hand firm on her waist. She felt neither the disgust she had with Mr. Bollinger nor the easy rapport she had felt with William. It was as though everything she had learned since coming to Wharton Manse had instantly disappeared, and once again, she felt the naive country girl, unschooled in the ways of Society.

"You are adapting to your new life here at Wharton Manse, Miss Royce?" Simon finally broke the silence, his deep voice vibrating through Charlotte's bosom where her breasts lightly brushed his chest.

Instantly at the sensation, she felt her nipples harden against the loose material of her bodice. She wondered if he could feel them and dared herself to look up into the hard lines of his face. His piercing hazel eyes pinned hers, and again, for a moment, she could do nothing but look into their depths as she felt her heart begin to race and her palms moisten, a blush heating her cheeks. Finally, she wrenched her gaze from his and looked back down at the safe button of his coat, worrying her lower lip between her teeth as she tried to ignore how good it felt to be in his arms.

What would she do if he looked at her with the same kind of hunger that she had seen in other men's eyes? The thought caused her to stumble slightly. Her embarrassment increased when she felt his hard thigh momentarily contact the pulsing heat between her legs as she struggled to regain the rhythm of the dance. Mortified by her clumsiness, she tried to pull back but felt his arm tighten about her waist, pulling her even more intimately to him.

"Easy, Miss Royce. Just follow my lead and you will be fine," he said.

Though the words were the same ones Mr. Bollinger had spoken to her, they had the opposite effect on her. Her legs grew weak and quivery as she felt her nipples press more firmly against his muscular chest, his hard thigh periodically rubbing her hot moist core at the juncture of her legs.

"I'm sorry, Sir Radway," she failed to keep the breathlessness from her voice. "I have only just learned the waltz." Her blush deepened at having to further reveal to him her lack of social polish.

"There is no need to apologize, Miss Royce. You are doing just fine for someone new to this activity." Though the timbre of his voice caused heated sensations to course through her, she couldn't help but stiffen slightly at the slightly paternal, condescending words he spoke.

She didn't want him to treat her as a graceless, unsophisticated country girl needing his reassurance. She remembered how William had looked at Barbara, even how Sir Prescott had looked at her earlier. She didn't want his pity, she realized. She wanted him to want her.

But the dance ended and he released her from his arms, giving her a formal bow before returning to join Sally, William and Barbara. She moved to the sideboard to pour another cool drink, when Mr. Bollinger seized her arm.

"You look overheated, my dear," he whispered in the repulsive, sibilant voice she was coming to detest. "Let us remove to the coolness of the out of doors."

Before she could object, he had propelled her outside and onto the terrace above the garden. She tried to wrench her arm free, but he seized both her arms and pushed her back against the stone ledge bordering the terrace.

"Be still, my girl. I won't hurt you." His lips were wet on the side of her neck as his hands forced hers back against the stone ledge.

She felt the stone jammed uncomfortably into the small of her back and she shuddered to feel him thrust his groin insinuatingly against hers.

"I will scream," she whispered frantically, feeling his wet mouth close over her nipple through the thin material of her bodice.

"You do and I will bite this off," he growled.

Her eyes widened with fear, instantly convinced that he meant what he said. As it was, the pressure of his teeth on her nipple was already causing her more pain than pleasure.

"Please," she fought not to beg, but fear took the upper hand. "Please let me go."

"Only if you promise to do as I say." He lifted his head to stare at her, his beady eyes slightly unfocused, his pupils dilated.

She nodded in response to his question, feeling defeated. She realized with dismay that he was drunk, his breath reeking of liquor. The man was irrational and violent, and she knew that no reasoning with him would work. Her only option was to go along with his demands until she could discover a way to escape.

"That's better, Miss Royce. I knew we would get along most amicably."

He took her arm and forced her with him down the steps and into the dark garden. In the moonlight, she could vaguely see that he had led her into the opening of the maze. He stumbled with her down one of the passages and then stopped at one of the maze's little clearings. Grabbing both her hands in one of his, with the other he quickly yanked her gown down to her waist, exposing her breasts.

"Beautiful," he said as his free hand roved across her, pressing and tweaking her nipples to hard tormented crests.

She closed her eyes, wishing herself away, somewhere far away, and had to bite back a cry of pain. Just when she thought she could stand it no more, she felt something soft twining about her wrists. Her eyes flew open to find him binding her hands with his cravat. She struggled to free her hands, but it was too late. They were tied tightly together at her waist.

"That's better," he whispered.

"What are you going to do?" She couldn't keep the terror from her voice as she saw him unbutton his pants.

"Take a seat, Miss Royce."

He pushed her onto the stone bench in the clearing and she gazed in revulsion and fear at his penis, pushing forward from the opening of his pants. Though it was dark, she could see that it lacked neither the stature nor the proportion of either William's or Sir Prescott's flesh. Short and stubby, it reminded her of Hornby the butler.

"Now sit still," he commanded.

She found his erect flesh coming closer, and for a moment, she feared he would demand she take him in his mouth as William had done. Instead, he seized her breasts once more in his hands, kneading them convulsively, his thumbs tweaking the nipples to hard, painful points. His legs forced her thighs open, spreading the material of her gown. and he stood between her legs. Unlike William, his shorter stature brought his flesh to the level of her breasts. Suddenly, she felt him jam his flesh between her breasts, his hands squeezing her breasts hard together to surround his penis. She shuddered in loathing but couldn't help but look down in appalled shock to see that he had buried himself between the deep valley of her breasts, his hands relentlessly tormenting her nipples. She closed her eyes, unable to stand the sight of him standing over her, and she did not want him to see the tears of humiliation and frustration that threatened to fall. She instinctively knew that such a man as Mr. Bollinger would enjoy the spectacle of a woman weeping.

"Oh yes, yes," he grunted, thrusting his hips rhythmically forward and backward, his penis pushing up and back through the cleft of her breasts. Despite her efforts to stop them, her tears were filling freely now, but she kept her eyes squeezed tight shut, clamping down on her lips to keep from screaming. Despite her efforts bailed and she let out a high-pitched keening cry for help.

"Bitch! Keep quiet!"

She felt his open hand slap her hard across the cheek. He grabbed her breasts again and the tempo of his thrusting increased, his hands like vises on her breasts. Too her disgust, she felt moisture seep from the tip of his flesh and lubricate its passage as it rubbed and then slid against her. Just when she thought the pain and humiliation would be too much and that she might lose consciousness, she suddenly felt Mr. Bollinger disappear.

"Ump!" She heard the sound of flesh being struck.

Her eyes flew open and in the moonlit darkness she saw a big man striking Mr. Bollinger once more in the gut. Mr. Bollinger collapsed and the man picked him up by the front of his shirt.

"You will leave now, Mr. Bollinger. Do not come back."

Charlotte gasped at the sound of that distinctive, deep and raspy voice. She would recognize Simon's authoritative voice anywhere. With help from the violent shove delivered by Simon, Mr. Bollinger stumbled back along the path of the maze toward Wharton Manse. Then, she found William's older brother standing over her.

"You are indisposed, Miss Royce?" He sounded concerned. His eyes traveled over her face and bared breasts, down to her tied hands.

She felt the hysterical urge to laugh. Was she indisposed? What kind of question was that to ask someone who had been taken captive, assaulted and mauled?

She hugged her shoulders together and with her bound hands tried to pull her bodice up, but it was impossible to cover herself. It had been humiliating enough for Mr. Bollinger to force his attentions on her, but it felt much worse now that Simon was there, seeing her so disheveled with tears streaming down her face. She cleared her throat to speak, but no words came. She looked up into his dark face, his eyes unreadable in the shadows.

"If I may, let me assist you," he said, though he seemed reluctant to take a seat beside her.

From the pocket of his trousers, he pulled a small penknife and quickly slit her bonds. As soon as her hands were free, she gathered her bodice together and tried to slip her arms back into the sleeves. Unwittingly, she glanced up at him and saw that he was staring at her bosom, her breasts still uncovered, swollen and erect from the torment Mr. Bollinger had inflicted. She wasn't able to interpret the cryptic look in his eyes. He looked at her neither with the sensual hunger of Sir Prescott and his brother nor with the predatory carnality of Mr. Bollinger and Hornby the butler. To her amazement, she realized she wanted him to look at her with some kind of masculine appreciation. Instead, he seemed reluctant to be at her side, perhaps even angry. Hastily, she covered her breasts, but she had trouble sliding her arms into the tight sleeves.

"Allow me," he said, his deep voice a quiet rasp.

His large, warm hands came to her first sleeve and pulled it back so she could slide in her arm. He repeated the gesture with the second sleeve. With each arm, she tried to tamp down the rising awareness she had of him as a man, sitting beside her in the dark garden, his hands grazing her chilled skin as he helped her.

Unlike her reaction to Mr. Bollinger, she was surprised to feel no fear of Simon, and in fact, she had to admit she wanted him to acknowledge her as a woman. As soon as she was properly garbed, however, he did not prolong their time together.

"Miss Royce, allow me to escort you indoors."

Rising to his feet, he held out his hand to her. She placed her hand in his and he helped her to her feet, but she was still unsteady after her ordeal. Stumbling, her legs threatened to give out on her.

"Careful," he said, and his arm encircled her waist as he pulled her against his side to keep her from falling.

The feel of his muscular body against hers caused a sensual fire to heat Charlotte's blood and she drew a shaky breath. He turned her to face him, his hands at her waist, and she stared helplessly up into the hard features of his face. His shoulder-length tawny hair had come loose from its queue in the struggle and a lock of it fell across the scar that marred his brow. She noted the high cheekbones, the strong jaw, and the determined lips. She knew instinctively that he was not bound by convention as Sir Prescott, nor dependent on others like William, nor victim of his own lusts like Mr. Bollinger. She realized that he was a real man, a maker of his own destiny.

"Thank-you for coming to my rescue, Sir Radway," she whispered.

"I was standing on the terrace smoking a cigar when I heard your cry out, Miss Royce. You are lucky that I found you when I did. Mr. Bollinger is a cad."

Charlotte nodded, tears forming again when she remembered what had happened earlier. She took a deep breath and realized that it was the aroma of cigar smoke that clung to his jacket. She had disliked the smell when Sir Prescott had smoked, but now, as the smoke combined with Simon's own subtle scent, it held an erotic, masculine allure. He was gazing down at her, his eyes traveling from her hair to her face. She noticed that he briefly glanced below to her cleavage but his eyes hurriedly returned to her face. His hands left her waist and came up to cup her cheeks. Charlotte could do nothing but stand breathlessly, waiting for the kiss that she knew was coming. But instead, to her vast disappointment, Simon's thumbs came up and brushed the tears from her eyes. He then smoothed her hair where it had become disordered during her struggle with Mr. Bollinger.

"Now you are presentable," he said, beginning to step away from her.

Charlotte didn't want this private, magic moment with him to end. Before she knew what she was doing, she stepped forward and reached up into his hair.

"Miss Royce?" His voice rumbled low in her ear and sent tremors of awareness through her body.

"Let me fix your hair," she breathed, shocked at her forwardness, and yet reveling in the feel of his thick hair sliding through her fingers.

Her action to resecure his queue brought her body close to his. Because of his height, she had to stand on her tiptoes and lean forward to reach the back of his head. He stepped back slightly, probably shocked at her wanton behavior, but his movement caused her to stumble forward and she suddenly found herself pressed against him, her hands firmly in his hair, her breasts mounded against his hard chest, her face resting against the warm curve of his neck.

"Miss Royce, please release me," he growled, but she detected a husky note in his voice that hadn't been there before.

"There, I'm done," she said, her fingers having nimbly resecured his hair in its tie.

She sought to pull back from him but discovered that his hands had closed on her waist and now held her captive. She felt her nipples erect into diamond points against the muscular wall of his chest.

"Sir?" She leaned her head back to look up at him.

In an instant, she saw that his earlier reluctant expression had disappeared. In its place was something fierce and savage and it made her pulse leap in response.

And then his head swooped down and she felt his lips moving over hers. Taking immediate advantage of her surprised gasp, his tongue slid forcefully inside her mouth and she forgot everything but the feel of him.

Sir Prescott had kissed her. William never had, she realized. But nothing had prepared her for the sensual onslaught of Simon's mouth on hers. It was as if he were drawing her very soul from her and setting it on fire to burn in an inferno of wanton need and desire. He could do anything to her and she would be his willing slave. She wanted him to take her breasts in his hands, in his mouth, and torment them as the other men had.

The image of him touching her as William had made her body writhe against him in pleasure, pushing her moist, pulsing core against him, seeking the press of his hard shaft against her. She felt the rigid length of him, big and erect against her, and the sensation made her lose all control. Her hands strayed from his hair to his back, and down to his hips, seeking to pull his turgid flesh closer to her desperate, throbbing heat.

"Miss Royce, compose yourself!"

Suddenly, she felt his hands hard on her shoulders, wrenching her away from him. Without his warmth, the night felt cold, and she felt her nipples jutting outward from the bodice of her gown.

She felt a slight satisfaction when she saw his eyes briefly stray there, but then his eyes returned to her face, his lips firm and his jaw clenched. She felt a wave of embarrassment sweep through her to think she had just flung herself at the man, but she refused to apologize for her behavior.

Instead, she wrapped her arms about herself and dropped her gaze, turning away from him.

"We should return, Sir Radway. The others will wonder what has become of us." She was dismayed to hear the quavery weakness in her voice and the prick of tears sting the back of her eyes.

"Of course, Miss Royce."

He quietly took her arm in his. No more words were spoken as he guided her back to Wharton Manse.

At the edge of the terrace, he paused, looking down at her.

"I think it best, Miss Royce, if we do not enter the room together. You had best enter first."

Charlotte nodded, gazing for one last, long moment up at him. The lights from the drawing room allowed her to better discern his features. In contradiction to the firm line of his mouth that was turned down almost into a frown, a hungry gleam still glinted in his hazel-green eyes. To her dismay, she felt her heart begin to race again.

She forced herself to turn away and, squaring her shoulders, marched into the drawing room, hoping that she looked composed. She quickly scanned the room as she entered it. Mr. Bollinger was seated with Mr. Geary and William at one end of the room, all three of them well on their way to complete inebriation. Barbara and Sally were seated at the other end of the room. The Horns and Mr. Singer must have retired to bed because they were no longer present.

"Oh, there you are, Charlotte," Barbara said as she took

a seat by the fire. "We were beginning to wonder what had happened to you."

"I wanted a breath of fresh air, so I took a turn in the garden." She studied Barbara for a moment, but there was nothing in her expression to indicate irony or ridicule.

"Did you happen to see Sir Radway while you were walking?" Sally asked, doing little to hide the jealous suspicion lacing her question.

Charlotte may not have been as sophisticated as the other women, but she had learned a few things since coming to Wharton Manse. She owed this woman no explanations and refused to let Sally intimidate here.

"No, I did not," she lied, priding her ability to keep from blushing. Just to be safe, however, she did not look at Sally when she answered the woman but kept her gaze on the fire.

Several moments later, she felt rather than saw Simon enter the drawing room. He immediately joined the drunken men at the bar. Rather than risk another interaction with the disgusting Mr. Bollinger or the intriguing Sir Radway, she decided it was time to make her escape. She whispered her good evenings to the ladies and then quietly exited the drawing room.

*****.

5 CHARLOTTE LEARNS TO YEARN

The next several days did not go well for Charlotte. Though she managed to avoid Mr. Bollinger's unwanted attentions, she found herself irresistibly, unacceptably drawn to Simon. He shared a family resemblance to William, but when she remembered her earlier dalliance with his brother, she found it impossible to believe that she had once thought William the most handsome of men. Compared to Simon, he was merely an effeminate boy still in leading strings.

Simon was a fully mature male, everything she could ever hope to desire for in a man. The situation was humiliating, because she saw how much Sally threw herself at the him and she had no wish for him to view her as he did Sally.

It didn't help that his continued polite rejections of Sally's advances gave her such smug satisfaction. When she thought of her engagement, her conscience pricked her and she began to look forward to her fiancé's return. Perhaps if Sir Prescott were there, his presence would break her fascinated obsession with Simon. At least, his being there would serve as a distraction. She could swear there were instances while in the breakfast room or in the evenings in the drawing room after dinner that she felt Simon's gaze on her.

During one of the card games, they had been seated beside each other and their hands touched when the cards were passed. His eyes had met hers and her breath caught in her throat, sure she saw that same glint in his eye she had seen after he kissed her. But later, as she sat in her rooms, she dismissed it all as the workings of her overheated imagination.

A large number of additional guests arrived for the upcoming festivities and Wharton Manse was in turmoil. Unused to so many strangers, Charlotte hid in her rooms. Sir Prescott was to return in another day and in the interim she kept herself entertained by reading books.

That afternoon, she finished the latest selection of books, so she carried them down to the library to pick out a few more. Most of the guests were out for the day visiting a neighboring estate, and Charlotte hoped she would have the library to herself.

She entered the room and placed the stack of books on one of the tables just inside the room. She turned around to close the door, when she was startled to find Simon rising from a seat in the corner by the window.

"Sir, I didn't see you." Her voice was husky with surprise. She felt paralyzed as she stood there, watching him approach her.

He moved with an agile grace that made her think of a big predatory cat. He was dressed today like she often saw him, in expensively simple, yet elegant attire. The day being warm, he had discarded his jacket on the chair where he had been reading. His crisp white shirt was cuffed at the wrists and he wore no neck cloth.

She felt her eyes drawn irresistibly to the curly chest hair she could see rising from the opening at his throat. Unconsciously, she clenched her hands in the folds of her skirt when she imagined running her hands across the hair on his hard chest. The tight fit of his black breeches emphasized the muscular length of his legs.

"Miss Royce, you are looking well today."

The familiar deep raspiness of his voice teased her with unwanted sensations. She firmly tried to squelch her errant thoughts and feelings, but looking up into the intensity of his hazel-green eyes made her efforts seem futile.

"Thank-you, sir," she said softly.

Though the yellow day dress she wore fit her snugly and showed her figure to advantage, she perversely found herself wishing it were evening and she was dressed in another of her ravishing gowns. She wanted him to want her. She wanted him to feel what she was feeling. Instead, their polite conversation continued.

"I would have thought that you would accompany the others to the Attleby Estate," he said.

He escorted her to a seat by the window.

"I thought likewise of you, Sir," she said, not realizing until after she uttered the words that they were an admission of her thinking about him.

A slight blush crept up her cheeks and she dropped her gaze from his. Besides a low chuckle, Simon did not comment.

"I have other, more important things to do besides socialize day in and day out, I'm afraid," he said. "Like your fiancé, Miss Royce, I am a busy man."

Something in his voice made her look up at him again. There was grim look about his mouth and he was focused intently on her.

"Sir?" she said, dropping her gaze, afraid of the severe look in his eyes.

"Miss Royce," he paused and cleared his throat. "I would like to apologize for the other night. You were the victim of that ignoble rake Bollinger and I took advantage of your situation."

"Sir—"

"Wait, please. Let me finish," he held his hand up as he

spoke. "I want to assure you that I hold your fiancé in the highest regard. Sir Prescott is a good friend and I would never do anything to dishonor him. You must know, too, Miss Royce, that I would never do anything to compromise you." He cleared his throat once more. "At least not intentionally," he added with a scowl.

"Of course, Sir, I trust you completely," she said hastily, wanting to relieve him of any distress he was feeling due to his behavior toward her. "You are a man of honor and loyalty, a very admirable man."

As she spoke the words, she found herself wishing he were maybe not so noble and honorable. Memories of their kiss swept through her and it felt as though his lips were once more pressed against hers, his tongue thrusting deep inside. A wave of heat at set fire to her body and she felt her nipples erect hard against the fine material of her high-necked gown. Her tongue crept out and she licked her lips, remembering the feel of him. She couldn't stop herself from gazing into the depths of his eyes. To her surprise, it was as though he were remembering their kiss as well. She saw his eyes shoot dark and intense; a heated color had risen high along his jaw.

He stood abruptly and walked stiffly away from her, keeping his back to her as he braced his arms against the desk.

"Miss Royce, you give me more credit than I am due. I am not so honorable nor so admirable as you say, but I do my best to remain loyal and respectful of my friends."

"Of course, Sir Radway," she said, unable to stop herself from admiring the muscular contours of his shoulders and back that stood out in sharp relief against his shirt, his muscles tight with tension.

She didn't know how to proceed. She knew that the proper thing would be for her to gather her new collection of books and leave the Earl to his studies, but what she really wanted to do was to walk over to him and rub his shoulders as William had done to her and ease the tension she could see radiating from him. She worried her lower lip between her teeth, pondering what to do.

Finally, she made her decision. Rising to her feet, she went to reclaim the books she had brought in. She carried the stack about the room and began reshelving them.

After a moment, Simon approached her and held out his hand.

"Here, let me assist you, Miss Royce," he said. "It's the least I can do." His smile was rueful as he took the stack from her.

"Thank-you, sir," she murmured.

For the next half hour, their interaction proved amicably polite. He asked her about her selection of books and they discussed their favorite works.

"I'm looking for Candide, but I haven't seen it here in Sir Prescott's collection," she said some time later.

She had laden Simon down with a pile of new books for her to read as he accompanied her about the library.

"I think it's up there." He inclined his head toward one of the higher shelves.

Charlotte slid the foot ladder over and nimbly climbed up. She didn't realize until she was at the top of the ladder and reaching for the volume that her position above Simon gave him an excellent view of her ankles and lower calves.

Startled at the thought, she lost her balance and began to fall. Instantly, Simon dropped the books and caught her in his arms.

"Simon!" she exclaimed, forgetting not to use his Christian name and gazing up into his eyes, watching them shoot dark with emotion.

"Charlotte," he breathed.

The next thing she knew, her arms had come around his neck, her hands burying themselves in his thick, tawny hair and loosening the queue.

She wasn't sure if it was she that pulled him to her or if it was his head that swooped down and met hers. Again, she experienced the fantastic sensations of him kissing her. She didn't hesitate but opened her mouth to him, her tongue eagerly ready to meet his in a sensual dual. He groaned, deep in his throat when he felt her tongue touch his, and she felt his hands move from her waist and up to the sides of her full breasts.

"Yes," she gasped, as his mouth left hers to travel to her ear and then down the side of her neck.

She let her head fall back giving him better access to her neck and bosom. How she wanted him to touch her there, where her nipples throbbed, her breasts jutting against his chest.

For too short a moment, she felt his large hands close over the aching mounds, his thumbs brushing their peaked crests. She felt the rock hard length of him push through the fine material of her dress to press against her moist, heated core.

"No, this is wrong!" He wrenched her back from him, his large hands hard on her shoulders putting some distance between their overheated bodies.

She could do nothing but stare at him, her eyes glazed, her body quivering with unfulfilled desire. She felt no shame or embarrassment as she had with the other men. She only felt the overwhelming desire to be back in his arms.

He was breathing unevenly, a hectic flush to his face and neck, and his hair flowed freely about his shoulders where she had loosened it like a mane. Her gaze dropped and she could see his raised flesh protruding large and weighty in sharp relief against the tight black breeches. She shifted her stance, unconsciously trying to relieve the pulsing dissatisfaction that throbbed between her legs.

He ground his teeth together, his hands clenched into fists at his sides. He took one more, long look at her, his gaze sweeping her body from head to toe, and then he turned away.

"Miss Royce, I am sure you will understand if I leave

you now," he ground out, his voice no more than a husky rasp.

"Yes, Simon," she said.

He paused briefly and she realized she had forgotten again not to use his Christian name. He walked jerkily to the library door and left the room.

Charlotte sank down on the floor beside the pile of books he had dropped in his effort to catch her. She didn't know why, but she felt tears stream down her face and suddenly she found herself crying as though her heart would break.

*****

6 CHARLOTTE TASTES ECSTASY

That night at dinner, Simon assiduously avoided Charlotte, and she noted with despair that he seemed a little more receptive to Sally's flirtations. Of course, there now three additional eligible girls added to the party. Miss Katherine Chelsea, Miss Dorothea Hanford, and Miss Rebecca Attleby were all beautiful, talented, and rich. If anything, they gave both Barbara and Sally a run for their money, flirting and sporting with William and his brother as well as Mr. Bollinger, who of all the men seemed to be most enjoying himself.

Charlotte was relieved that Mr. Bollinger's attentions were directed elsewhere, but it frustrated her to no end that Simon could so easily build a fortress of pretty girls about him to keep her at a distance. She forced herself to play hostess to the new guests that had arrived, many of the older couples close friends with Sir Prescott.

As she listened to another lady's complaint of rheumatism, she had to admit to herself that she was not looking forward to becoming Sir Prescott's wife. The idea of having to entertain so many elderly ladies and listen to their bodily ills, or worse yet, to hear of their schemes to marry off their granddaughters by giving them Seasons in

Town, made her realize how vast the difference in age was between Sir Prescott and herself. When she compared him to Simon, she couldn't believe that she had agreed to marry him, much less let him touch her.

When Mr. Singer struck up a waltz on the piano, the younger guests enthusiastically began to dance. Charlotte sat at the side with the older folks, barely listening to the ramblings of Lady Bernadette about her grandson's case of croup. Instead, she watched the bright colors of the young ladies in the arms of the younger gentlemen swirl past her. Miss Dorothea Hanford was in Simon's arms, her eyes sparkling and her face radiant as she laughed at something the Earl said. Charlotte hated herself for the sharp stab of envy she felt, knowing that what she was feeling was wrong and that she was dishonoring her engagement to Sir Prescott. But she couldn't help it.

Several dances later, she found William bending over her hand. "I hope you will give me the pleasure of accepting a dance with me, Miss Royce?"

When Charlotte shook her head to dismiss him, wanting only to dance with his brother, Lady Bernadette elbowed her none too gently. "You get along, gel. A step or two on the dance floor would do you some good."

So, Charlotte let William draw her into his arms and sweep her about the floor.

"Where have you been, Miss Royce? The last few days, you seem to have disappeared. I was so hoping to continue our lessons."

She glanced briefly up into his midnight blue eyes, again comparing his flawless good looks with his brother's. His eyes wandered down to the deep cleavage of her dark red gown. She had taken extra care to dress for dinner, hoping to draw Simon's attention with this particularly seductive dress. But it hadn't worked. Instead, it seemed she had only managed to lure his brother.

"Why, Mr. Hathaway, I thought you had your hands full," she giggled coyly, casting a pointed glance at Barbara who was dancing for once with her own, portly and elderly husband.

Charlotte batted her eyelashes at William. He no longer intimidated her, and she realized that he had lost his power over her. He grinned down at her, the arm about her waist pulling her closer.

"You are a delectable temptress, my dear," he said, his other hand caressing the tender flesh at her wrist.

As his long legs moved between hers in the steps of the dance, she felt his penis press lightly against her stomach. At the sensation, she thought of his brother and realized that her body fit so much better within Simon's arms. She looked over William's shoulder and met Simon's gaze. He was dancing with Miss Katherine Chelsea, but his eyes were on her, watching her within his brother's arms. She saw the hard line of his jaw as he clenched his teeth and she saw how his eyes darkened as he watched them. It was obvious he disapproved of William's attentions to her.

Perhaps it was out of spite or perhaps it was because she wished him to feel as frustrated and powerless as she, but she gave him a suggestive little smile and then wantonly thrust her breasts against his brother's chest.

"Why, Miss Royce, does this mean you would like to resume your lessons with me?"

"Oh no, Mr. Hathaway, I realize you are much too busy for that," she simpered, snuggling closer to his tall form. "I simply love the feel of dancing with you."

The dance ended, but before William could return her to her seat and as Mr. Singer struck up the next waltz on the piano, Charlotte found herself abruptly swept into Simon's arms.

The feel of him holding her against his muscular body was glorious and her eyes swept shut for an instant as she let herself fully experience the moment. When she opened them, she looked up to see him staring hungrily down at her, his hazel-green eyes dark and intense.

"You should stay away from my brother, Miss Royce,"

he said, his deep voice resonating through her body.

She couldn't stop the little thrill of pleasure that pulsed through her as her breasts pressed into his chest, her nipples hard against him. She saw his eyes momentarily dip to her deep cleavage and she realized that he could feel the full swell of her breasts.

Abandoning any attempts at modesty, she thrust her jutting breasts more firmly against him, relishing the raspy feel of the material moving sensuously across her distended nipples. As their limbs moved in rhythm to the dance, she felt his penis harden and push periodically against her abdomen. The sensation was tantalizing and promised of so much more. She couldn't help the moisture she felt pooling between her thighs, and her legs began to quiver in reaction.

"Sir Radway, I see no reason to do such a thing as stay away from your brother. He is pleasant and chivalrous. He is a true gentleman," she said, knowing she was baiting him, but she drew a certain satisfaction in pushing him to his limits as he had done to her the past few days with his flirtatious behavior with the other women.

"My brother, Miss Royce, is a confirmed rake," Simon ground out. "He is not safe company for someone such as yourself."

This was too much for Charlotte, and she glared up at him, her blue eyes flashing.

"Sir, am I to take it that you think I am merely some naive and unsophisticated country girl? Do you think that if that were true Sir Prescott would have deigned to marry me?"

She saw his eyes widen in surprise at her words. She couldn't help adding fuel to the fire, so she said, "Or, Simon," she used his Christian name with dramatic emphasis, "should I take your warning to me about your brother as a sign that you are jealous?"

She had the satisfaction of seeing fury spark in his eyes, but she was unprepared when he swung her in a series of deft swooping moves out through the open French doors and onto the terrace. She found that he had taken her to the darkest corner of the landing, an alcove at the far end, enclosed with potted plants and shrubs and hidden out of sight of the drawing room. His hands were clamped hard on her upper arms. She looked up at him and, just for a moment, she was frightened by the savage and dangerous glint in his eyes.

"Perhaps I was wrong about you, Miss Royce," he spat out her name. "Let's just see, shall we?"

The next thing she knew, he was kissing her, violently, his mouth assaulting hers with such force that she felt his teeth grind against his. She gasped and his tongue swooped into her mouth, plundering hers with an intensity that made her feel like she would either melt or swoon in his arms. To keep from doing either, she wrapped her arms about his neck and speared her fingers through his thick hair, yanking it free from the restraints of the queue.

The kiss went on and on, his lips and mouth establishing a rhythm with hers that set her body on fire. He pushed her body back against the wall of the alcove and the next thing she knew, he had forced a muscular thigh between her legs, spreading them wide. His hands closed on her waist, lifting her, and she gasped to feel him settle her on his thigh. The sensitive juncture between her legs rubbed tortuously against the long hard length of his thigh and for a moment she was reminded of the horseback ride she had taken with his brother. It was as though she were riding his thigh. The sensation was glorious and achingly unsatisfying at the same time.

"Please," she whispered against his neck as his mouth dropped to the rising swell of her breasts.

"Please what, Miss Royce?" His voice feathered over her tender flesh.

She shivered as she felt his hands lower her bodice and free her breasts. Finally, she had the satisfaction she had craved, his mouth closing over an aching nipple, his one hand molding and caressing a breast, his other hand moving to her buttocks and pressing her more firmly against his thigh.

He slid her back and forth along the length of his thigh, the friction causing a flame that grew into a wildfire that suddenly exploded.

"Oh heavens!" she cried, startled as pleasure ripped through her, causing spasms of release.

She collapsed against him, her face pressed to his firm chest. She could feel his heartbeat racing under the damp, heated material of his shirt. He leaned back and lifted her chin with his big hand.

"Well, well, well, Miss Royce," he said, his eyes dark as he took in her flushed face and swollen lips. "I guess I was wrong about you after all."

He swept her up into his arms. She lay passively against him, still recovering from the ecstasy he had given her. She only vaguely registered that he had vaulted the ledge of the terrace and had carried her deep into the depths of the maze.

"Where are you taking me?" she said, when she realized how far they had gone.

Her bodice lay still about her waist, her breasts exposed and growing cold in the night air. She made to straighten her gown, but he stayed her with the husky sound of his voice.

"Stay as you are, Miss Royce. We have arrived."

He set her down and she realized they must be at the center of the maze. A flowery bower surrounded a gazebo. He took her hand and guided her into the structure. She saw that it housed several couches and cushioned seats. She felt the night chill and again sought to pull up her gown.

"No, Miss Royce, we are not finished yet."

He came to stand beside her, his hands moving now without reserve over her bare breasts, cupping their large mounds, his thumbs teasing their crests into throbbing rigid peaks. He stared intently down into her face and then dropped his gaze to look at his hands on her tender flesh.

"Sir?" she murmured, her voice made breathless by the feel of his hands on her. She knew not what he intended, but she realized she trusted him and wanted whatever he planned to do.

"Let me pleasure you," he rasped, his voice deep and commanding.

"Yes," she sighed as she felt his mouth take her breast again, and she felt the moisture and desperate heat build between her thighs once more. She speared her hands into his hair, jutting her breasts up to meet his ardent mouth. She felt his raised flesh push persistently against her abdomen, and with one hand, she reached down to touch it.

"No, Miss Royce," he growled, seizing her hand in his and bringing it to his chest.

Denied that pleasure, she swiftly unbuttoned his shirt and wriggled her hand through the opening, reaching in to stroke his crisp chest hair, her thumb teasing his masculine nipple as he teased hers with his lips and tongue.

"You are full of surprises, Miss Royce," he exhaled and she gasped in surprise as he turned her away from him, his hands on her hips.

"On your hands and knees," he whispered in her ear, pushing her down against the cushions of the couch.

She complied, not knowing what he intended, feeling her breasts swing heavily forward with the motion.

His hands were warm on her thighs and she realized he had raised her skirts about her waist. She felt his hands massage the rounded flesh of her buttocks and she couldn't stop the moan that issued from her throat. His hands wandered across her bare behind and then one of them dipped to her moist core. She gasped again as he spread her thighs wide and she felt him kneel between her parted legs.

"Yes, Miss Royce, you are full of surprises," he said.

One of his hands reached up to mold and caress her breast, his thumb and forefinger squeezing her nipple and causing frissons of pleasure to arc through her. His other hand toyed with her below. His mouth chewed on her ear, his tongue teasing its inner recesses.

"Now, Miss Royce, let us finish this little game," he groaned.

She felt something large, hot and hard press against her at the tender junction of her thighs. It seemed huge and blunt, much, much bigger than William's fingers had been. The pressure built and released against her moist core as she felt Simon move rhythmically against her, and she suddenly realized it was his penis and that he was going to put himself inside her.

But it felt too big! Terror gripped her. She had seen how large William's penis had been. Sir Prescott's had not seemed much smaller. She couldn't see Simon's, but it felt enormous.

"No, Sir, no," she whispered, tensing in fear.

But it was too late.

With a strong surging thrust, Simon ripped through her maidenhead and plunged himself into her. She let out a loud, keening scream, cut off abruptly by the pressure of his hand clamping over her mouth.

"Good God, woman!" he exclaimed. He paused, his body buried deep inside her. "You are — were — a virgin."

His breath came hot and uneven in her ear, and she could feel his flesh pulsing deep inside her as he lay motionless over her. Her body burned and seared where he impaled her.

She couldn't see his face because hers was pushed ignominiously into the cushions, but she could hear the shock in his voice. Abruptly, she realized the humiliation of her position, her body bent over on hands and knees, Simon crouched above her. They were like rutting animals. It was most shameless and indecent.

"Get off me, Sir, this instant," she said, trying to hide the embarrassment and pain she felt with outrage. She tried to push back against him , but that served only to thrust his rigid flesh deeper into her throbbing core.

"No, Miss Royce — Charlotte. I'm afraid I can't yet do that." He froze for a moment, his voice a barely intelligible rasp, and then she felt one of his hands move to the front of the tender junction between her thighs. He began to rub her there, gently, tantalizingly. The hard length of him filling her seemed to sensitize her tender flesh and the incessant motion of his hand caused her to begin to writhe helplessly against him, the pain of his initial entry dissipating on a wave of pleasure.

"Yes, Charlotte, yes," he breathed into her ear, keeping himself still inside her, but the motion of her writhing against him caused her to slide sensuously along his long thick length. He groaned and shifted, moving his hand to tease and squeeze her nipple and then cup the heavy weight of her breast as it swung with their combined movement.

For an instant, she remembered William's fingers in her and how she had longed for more. Now she knew what she had craved. The feel of Simon filling her with his massive, engorged flesh caused a fire to build anew inside her. She could not bite back the moan of pleasure as she felt him withdraw and then move himself relentlessly back into her tight depths. The pain had fled and now the fire burned, the sensation of his hand rubbing her between her legs, his other hand squeezing her breast to an aching awareness, his lips hungry against her neck, his hot, turgid length surging into her, caused a mounting pressure to build.

"Oh please," she panted, pleading for release.

She writhed against him again, wanting something she new not what, but he continued his measured assault on her body, his tempo steady and unceasing as he thrust into her, endlessly fanning the flames higher and higher, her body feeling as if it was about to fly apart.

"Yes," she screamed as explosions of ecstasy ripped through her and she fell against the cushions.

She was only vaguely aware of his hands hard on her hips, holding her steady as he pistoned himself into her, ramming himself deep into her in a rapid rhythm and then letting out a guttural groan as he collapsed over her, his body enfolding hers where she lay pressed into the cushion.

Charlotte had no idea how much time passed. It was as though she had lost consciousness, Simon's body like a warm blanket covering her, his flesh still buried deep within her, a pungent and cooling moisture seeping down the side of her thigh.

Suddenly, she opened her eyes, realizing what they had done. He had compromised her!

"Simon! Sir Radway!" She pushed back against him, trying to wriggle free.

His arm swept around her waist and to her shock, she felt him swell inside her, filling her again with his large and thick, turgid length.

"Charlotte, mmmm," he sighed, his mouth coming to her ear again, one of his hands straying to cup and mold her breast.

"Simon, this must stop. Don't you realize what we have just done?"

"Yes, Charlotte. I know what I have done. I have thoroughly and completely compromised you."

He shifted his body and rotated her in his arms. She found herself now on her back, pinioned under him, her legs spread wide, his body positioned between them, his flesh massively engorged and throbbing deep inside her.

Heaven help her, but as she looked up into his dark, dilated eyes, she felt desire build again, pulsing through her body.

"The damage is done, Charlotte, so forgive me if I steal

one more moment of pleasure from you," he grunted, taking a breast in his mouth and thrusting his hips hard against hers, pistoning his jutting penis rhythmically into her once more.

This position was so much more intimate, she thought distractedly, as she registered the maelstrom of passion flashing across his face.

His shirt hung open and she reached up to flick her hands across his flat nipples.

"Yes," she sighed, giving into sensation.

His hands grabbed her buttocks to more deeply penetrate her, the rhythmic pounding of his flesh into hers tearing down the last remnant of her resistance. She screamed her release into his mouth as he took hers in a deep drugging kiss. His large muscular body reached a frenzied tempo, plunging into her, and then he obtained his own release.

Moments later, she found herself seated on the cushion of the couch in the gazebo, her thighs spread wide as he sat between them, brushing a handkerchief against her.

"I must apologize, Miss Royce," he said, his expression rueful. "I have made a terrible miscalculation."

He finished dabbing at the moisture between her thighs and then pulled her skirts down over her legs. He moved to sit beside her and help her pull her bodice up over her breasts but not before dropping a last lingering kiss on her left breast.

She shivered helplessly with awareness, her body instantly on fire for him again. He refused to look her in the eyes, and she realized perhaps he was afraid he might see desire there. Perhaps, she wondered, if he saw how her renewed desire he would be unable to restrain himself.

"Don't you think, Simon, it's a little late to use such formalities as calling me 'Miss Royce,'" she said, her voice little more than a whisper.

He did not look at her but kept his gaze trained on the dark bower beyond the gazebo.

"Charlotte, I thought based on what you said earlier that you were a woman of experience."

"What do you mean? I said no such thing." She was shocked and dismayed that he would blame her for what had happened between them.

"You implied that Sir Prescott proposed to you because you were not an innocent country girl."

"What?" she said, refusing to acknowledge what she had said.

"And you can't deny how you were carrying on with my brother, can you?" He persisted. "You must know that William is a terrible rake. You must know of his dalliance with Barbara. Everyone does."

"So what does any of that have to do with what just happened between us?"

"I thought you were a woman of experience. Based on what you said, I thought you had already tasted the pleasures of marital relations with Sir Prescott. And when I saw you in William arms, I thought you were engaged in a dalliance with my brother."

She jumped to her feet and began hurrying back through the maze. He followed close on her heels and took her arm

"Wait," he said.

She turned on him. "I don't understand you, Simon. You accuse me of being some kind of wanton harlot, carrying on with your brother at the same time I am engaged to my fiancé. So why would you want me? Are you drawn to wanton harlots?" She dashed the tears from her eyes and tore away from him and ran down the path.

"Not that way," he grabbed her by her arm again and easily swung her about to face him. With his free hand, he cupped her chin and brought her face up to his.

"I don't think you're a harlot," he said earnestly. "It's just that I had no wish to compromise you or to jeopardize my friendship with your fiancé. Because of what I have done, you are no longer a virgin. Damn it, what a muddle," he broke off, running his hands distractedly through his hair. "We must get back to the party, before anyone realizes that we are missing. I hope it is not too late, already," he said, guiding her quickly through the shrubbery.

At the edge of the maze, he turned to her once more. "I think it best if no one sees you right now."

He brushed a strand of hair from her eyes, taking in her swollen lips and the tears staining her cheeks.

"Go up the servants' stairs to your rooms. If for whatever reason people ask about you and if it's necessary, I can make mention that you retired due to a headache."

The idea of facing everyone else was too much. Charlotte was thankful that he took charge of the situation. She nodded, too tired and emotionally wrung out to do anything but comply. He pressed a quick kiss to the back of her hand and then hurried out of the maze and up the stairs to the terrace. On weak legs, she stumbled to the back door of Wharton Manse.

Fortunately, she managed to reach her rooms unseen. Once in her rooms, she struggled free of her gown and corset without requesting help from Alice. She did not want the maid to see her. Pulling the nightgown over her, she collapsed across the bed, her body wrung out but still quivering with sensation. As she lay there, she felt the cooling trickle of moisture seep down her thighs, her body still burned slightly where he had so thoroughly taken her maidenhead. She sighed and the scent of him filled her nostrils. Helplessly, she felt a pulsing desire begin to throb through her again. She punched the pillow as she sought sleep.

*****

.

7 CHARLOTTE LEARNS A NEW LESSON

For a moment the next morning, Charlotte remembered nothing of the night before. She stretched languorously against the sheets, the sensation of her sheer nightgown sliding against her body felt voluptuous and stimulating. Her hand came up to stroke her full breast, its size now easily overflowing her hand, and she sighed in pleasure, feeling her nipple crest against her fingers. Her other hand slid between her thighs.

What was she doing!

Abruptly, she sat up and pulled a pillow against her chest. And then she remembered. Simon had compromised her. The memories of him touching her, filling her with his thick and long, throbbing flesh, caused a hectic blush to heat her face. Heavens, what had she done? Her mind raced frantically over the situation. William had toyed with her, but he had not compromised her. Sir Prescott had also been careful to keep her innocence intact. Simon had done no such thing. He had pierced lustily through her maidenhead and fully taken his pleasure. She was no longer a virgin. The thought filled her with alarm. Sir Prescott expected to marry a virgin. She realized in an instant that she must never let Sir Prescott know what had transpired between Simon and herself. It would be the only way to ensure their marriage would take place and that her family would be kept safe from destitution.

A knock sounded on the door.

"Miss Charlotte, ye be awake?" Alice called to her.

"Yes, Alice. Come in." She lay back among the pillows, pulling the covers to her chin and hoping that she looked suitably innocent.

The maid entered carrying a breakfast tray.

"Lady Geary said you would be wanting breakfast in bed, seeing as you have a headache and all."

"That is very kind of Barbara, but I feel quite fine."

She forced herself out of bed. It was obvious that Simon had had to resort to the lie last night. Under no circumstances did she want to risk suspicion about the time he spent with her.

"Help me dress," she told Alice.

The breakfast room was crowded with the guests. Charlotte managed to inconspicuously move to the sideboard and help herself to the poached eggs. As she poured herself a cup of coffee, Barbara approached her.

"So you are feeling better this morning, Charlotte?"

"Much," she said, hoping she sounded as casual as Barbara did.

"We just received word that Edmund is returning this afternoon," Barbara said.

Charlotte's heart beat with alarm, but she managed a polite smile. "How excellent, I do so miss my fiancé."

She took her plate and cup of coffee and moved away from Barbara. Seeing the Horns and Lady Bernadette, she retreated to the safety of a seat at their table. Surreptitiously, as she ate her breakfast, she glanced about the room. Most of the other ladies flitted about. William and Mr. Bollinger were there. She wasn't sure if she were disappointed or relieved to see that Simon was not among the guests.

As if reading her mind, Mr. Horn spoke to Lady Bernadette.

"Mr. Geary and Sir Radway are presently at the Attleby Estate purchasing new horseflesh to add to Sir Prescott's stables."

"Very good. The hunt promises to be a dashing affair," Lady Bernadette said with relish. "Do you ride, Miss Royce?" Caroline Horn asked Charlotte.

Charlotte breathed a sigh of relief when the rest of breakfast proceeded without incident. She began to relax, thankful that no one seemed the wiser about the change of her condition.

***

"My sweet, did you miss me?" Sir Prescott wrapped his tall, lean form about Charlotte, giving her a close hug.

They stood outside the front of Wharton Manse surrounded by guests, including Simon. Sir Prescott had just descended the carriage and taken her into his arms. She couldn't stop the blush that heated her cheeks, knowing that Simon was there, watching her. Sir Prescott leaned back and chuckled when he saw her embarrassment, mistaking her discomfiture for modesty.

"I am glad," he said, answering his own question and placing a quick kiss on her lips. He then turned to address his guests.

"Welcome everybody to Wharton Manse. I hope you have all been well situated and are enjoying yourselves." Taking Charlotte's arm, he led the crowd inside. "Let us have some tea."

The drawing room spilled over with guests onto the terrace as people sipped their tea and enjoyed an array of Wharton's finest pastries. The sun cast a glow across the granite terrace warming those who chose to gather out of doors. Sir Prescott kept Charlotte close at his side, his arm tucked in hers as they made the rounds among the guests.

"You have met the Horns, my dear? They are some of my closest friends," he said, guiding her to where the Horns were seated.

"Yes," she murmured and made small talk with Sir Prescott's elderly friends.

Again and again she blushed to think that Simon was among the guests, watching as Sir Prescott touched her and occasionally pressed intimate kisses to the side of her neck. Fortunately, Sir Prescott mistook her blushes for modesty.

"Wait until we are alone, my sweet," he whispered in her ear, and again she felt a blush heat her face.

This time, it was because Simon's piercing hazel-green eyes were trained on them, watching intently as Sir Prescott tucked his arm more closely around her waist. She saw how his nostrils flared and his eyes flashed. It thrilled her to know how much he disliked seeing Sir Prescott touch her, but there was nothing she could do except allow the older man's caresses. He was her fiancé, after all.

Eventually, the dreaded moment came when Sir Prescott escorted her to where Simon stood in the sun on the terrace. He was flanked by William on one side and Sally on the other. Charlotte forced herself to maintain a bland expression, though inwardly she seethed to see Sally clinging to Simon's arm, the woman's pert breast so obviously thrust against him.

"Welcome, Simon, I hope you are enjoying your stay," Sir Prescott moved forward to clasp his friend's hand. "You have met my fiancé, Miss Charlotte Royce?"

Charlotte couldn't meet Simon's gaze. Instead, she trained her eyes on the top button of his coat.

"I have indeed had the pleasure, Sir Prescott. Miss Royce."

She bit her bottom lip hard to keep from showing any

emotion as he took her suddenly damp hand in his and pressed a gentlemanly kiss on the back of it.

"You are a lucky man, my friend," he said, giving her hand a quick squeeze before releasing it.

A wave of heat swept through her at the secret contact. She forced herself not to look at him but turned her gaze to William, who Sir Prescott was now addressing.

"Bonnie tells me that you were kind enough to keep my Charlotte company for a few days."

Charlotte was surprised to hear the cold tone in Sir Prescott's voice. She glanced up at him and saw that his face was set in rigid lines.

"Your cousin was most insistent, Sir, that your fiancé not be left alone. I was happy to abide by Lady Geary's request."

William's words were smooth and Charlotte was astounded to see how he could pass off his dalliance with her as though nothing had happened. She realized she still had a lot to learn about how to conduct herself with worldly aplomb. As she noted Sir Prescott's suspicious glances at William, she couldn't help but see that it was to her advantage that he suspected nothing between herself and Simon. In fact, as he escorted her to the next set of guests, he whispered in her ear.

"It looks like the Earl of Radway is soon to have a Lady Radway." He had assumed that Sally and Simon were an item. She couldn't help but breathe a sigh of relief.

***

Her relief was short-lived, however, when she retired upstairs to dress for dinner. Within seconds of her retiring, a knock sounded on her door.

"Come in," she called, and found Sir Prescott stalking into the room.

He had a dark expression clouding his black eyes. He came to stand behind her where she sat at the vanity, brushing out her waist-length blond hair.

She looked up at him in the mirror.

"Sir?" she said, feeling his hands close hard on her shoulders.

"I need to speak with you about something, Charlotte."

His voice sounded serious, and for an instant, she was terrified that somehow he had discovered her transgression with Simon. She turned to face him.

"What is it?" she asked, her heart beating heavily in her chest.

"Is there anything you want to tell me about Mr. Hathaway?" he said.

She looked up at him, biting her lower lip.

"I'm not sure what you mean, sir." she said.

"Drat that man!" he exclaimed.

Abruptly, she found herself pulled out of the chair and against Sir Prescott's tall, lean body. He wrapped his arms around her, one hand tight in her hair to yank her head back, and then he sunk his mouth against hers. She opened in passive submission as his tongue thrust into her mouth. It was all she could do to keep the shudder of revulsion from noticeably ripping through her.

Fleetingly, she remembered Simon's violent assault on her mouth, but there was no comparison. Where Simon had tasted of port, cigar, and a heady male passion, Sir Prescott's thin lips and darting tongue felt reptilian, the intimacy of the kiss appalling. He seemed to sense her lack of response and pulled back.

"I am sorry, my dear," he murmured, running a hand through his gray hair. "I had no right to manhandle you thusly."

She didn't know what to say, so she stood silently beside him. He took her arm and guided her to the bed. Seating himself, he pulled her onto his lap.

"I missed you, my sweet, and I am behaving like a jealous cad. For a moment, I thought Mr. Hathaway had behaved improperly with you."

He quickly unbuttoned the front of her daydress, freeing her breasts and taking a nipple in his mouth. Repeatedly, he lathed it with his tongue, bringing it to an erect peak. With one hand, he molded and tweaked her other nipple to aching awareness, his other hand caressing the curve of her hip.

She fought the sensations he was invoking in her body, but then she realized she was being absurd. She was engaged to this man, and it was only right and proper that he should touch her. She couldn't help moving sensuously as his touch expertly elicited a response from her body.

"Maybe we have time before dinner for a little more instruction," he muttered against her breast, his hands pulling her skirt up over her thighs.

He glanced up and saw the embarrassed look on her face. Again it worked to her advantage. He mistook her shame at an old man fondling her as a blush of naiveté.

"I don't know what I was thinking, my sweet. Of course, you would not let someone of Mr. Hathaway's ilk touch you. You are so young, so untouched, my sweet," he sighed.

His long bony hand crept up her thigh and teased the flesh surrounding her moist core.

"Do you like that? Does that feel good?" he asked, his mouth suckling again on her distended nipple.

She gasped, unable to stop her body from responding to his persistent manipulations. She nodded, mutely, and she felt his smile against her breast.

"Good, my dear. Very good."

She felt his penis raised and hard, pressing against her side, and she wondered for a moment if he was planning to claim his husbandly rights before their marriage day. Fear swept through her to think that if he did he might discover she was no longer a virgin. The thought of him inside her caused her to shudder with disgust.

His hand fumbled with his breeches and her eyes flew to his when she saw that he had freed his penis. It rose long and erect between them. She saw that it was shorter than William's and much thinner. She realized that she had never actually seen Simon's penis, though she had felt it inside her, its massive length filling her with delicious fulfillment. The memory made moist heat instantly pool between her thighs.

Sir Prescott's roving fingers felt the moisture and he rubbed it against the sensitive nub of flesh at the juncture of her thighs. She wriggled under his ministrations, uncontrollable heated tension building within her.

"See how I want you, my sweet?" He gripped his penis with one hand. Seeing the fear in her eyes, he continued. "Don't worry, my dear. I promise that this is only a lesson in love. Think of it as preparation for our wedding night. Now, touch me. Yes," he sighed, guiding her hand to wrap around his veiny flesh.

She stroked him as he had taught her.

"Yes, that is good," he crooned. And then he rose to his feet in front of her. "Let's see. What lesson shall I teach you next?"

He looked down at her for a long moment, gazing at her breasts and her pink flesh exposed to him where her skirts pushed up about her waist, the rosy blush coloring her cheeks, her eyes darkened slightly with fear. She wondered for a moment if he intended for her to take him in her mouth and she shivered. Instead, a small smile played across his lips.

"Turn around, my dear, and lie on the bed."

She complied, wondering what he had planned for her.

"Now, lift your skirts for me. Higher. More. That's good."

She felt the cool air of the room waft across the bare skin of her buttocks. She felt Sir Prescott's hands spreading her legs wide and tilting her hips upward slightly.

Instantly, she remembered Simon and how he had first made love to her. The memory caused a wildfire of heat to flare through her, her nipples erecting against the bed sheets where her breasts pushed into them, her mouth moist against the pillows.

Sir Prescott's hands traveled up her legs and inner thighs. She felt his fingers graze the moist passage between her legs and then caress and mold the plump mounds of her buttocks. He rhythmically squeezed her buttocks, pushing them together and then separating the lobes.

"Do you like that, my sweet? Does that feel good?" She heard him ask, his breath coming unevenly behind her.

"Yes," she said, realizing she spoke the truth.

There was something sensual and almost hypnotic in the way that he repeatedly stroked and caressed her buttocks, his hand occasionally wandering around underneath her to tease the sensitive nub of flesh. She felt his long, lean body climb over her, the material of his breeches scraping along the tender skin of her inner thighs. His hands traveled between her buttocks and then up to her breasts, squeezing her nipples to aching points.

"Yes, very good, my sweet," he crooned in her ear, his breathing accelerating and growing even more unsteady.

He was lying over her and she could feel his hot, raised flesh pressing between the lobes of her ass. There was something embarrassing, humiliating about what he was doing. It seemed so improper, a man of his age lying atop her. But then one of his hands moved under her to caress her sensitive nub and the other repeatedly squeezed and released her throbbing nipple.

He thrust his veiny penis between the lobes of her ass, the movement pushing her body down into the bed and more firmly against his rubbing fingers. The action reminded her for a moment of Mr. Bollinger and how he had pressed his penis between her breasts. Her body had felt cold and used by that disgusting man.

Now, she was embarrassed to discover that her body would so wantonly respond to Sir Prescott's ministrations, especially when she no longer found the man attractive.

Suddenly, she imagined that it was Simon lying over her and not a man old enough to be her grandfather. A wave of pleasure swept through her as she imagined Simon encompassing her with his body.

She writhed sensuously against the sheets. Sir Prescott felt her movement and groaned.

"Yes, that's right. Now, I will show you something new, something exquisite."

She felt his penis poke against the tight bud of her bottom. She realized he meant to penetrate her there, of all places. The idea was revolting. She struggled to twist away from him, but his hands grabbed her hips firmly, holding her steady.

"No!" she cried, but he pushed her face into the soft pillows.

"Relax, my dear." His voice was a sibilant hiss against her ear, his lips leaving a wet trail from her ear to her neck.

She shuddered. His hands returned to caressing her breasts and the sensitive nub between her legs, his penis remained buried between the lobes of her ass, pressing against the tight opening.

"It will be much better if you relax. Yes," he said, feeling the moisture seep from her as he rubbed her nub mercilessly.

She squirmed, and the action forced his penis a little deeper within her. She quivered at the sensation, shocked and appalled to think that he was penetrating her there of all places, but his hands would not stop their continuous torment of her body, and the tension continued to build.

"Yes, yes," he groaned, sliding himself slowly, further into her tight depths.

With each movement inward of his hard flesh, Charlotte moaned with pain. But then he would pause, his body pulsing inside her as he waited, and she would find her body stretching to accommodate him. She tried not to think of a man old enough to be her grandfather doing what he was to her body. She forced herself to imagine it was Simon pushing himself into her. She moved slightly against him.

"Yes!" he groaned, his hands increasing their tempo as they rubbed her sensitized flesh and squeezed her breasts.

He sunk himself fully into her. Charlotte couldn't stop the moan of near pain at his deep intrusion. He remained buried in her, his penis motionless except for its rhythmic pulsating.

"How is that, my sweet? Is that pleasant?" he crooned in her ear.

His finger slid into her moist core as he slowly withdrew his penis from her tight passage, and he then sunk himself into her once more, his finger moving back and forth inside her in the front, his thumb rubbing the sensitized nub at the juncture of her thighs, his other hand squeezing the tender mound of her buttocks as he withdrew and then pushed his rigid flesh into her again.

She couldn't stop the violent sensations building in her body and she writhed sinuously under him, feeling violated yet titillated at the same time.

"Sir!" she cried, her voice muffled in the pillows as she felt her body convulse around his finger where it moved inside of her, her breasts beading to diamond hard points, her body split asunder by his intimate violation of her backside.

"Yes!" he cried and plunged himself a final time into her tight passage.

She felt his full weight for a moment as he shuddered against her, releasing himself. She was thankful to feel the almost instant wilting and retreat of him from her body, grateful he had not Simon's stamina nor Simon's girth.

She lay inert on the bed, her face still buried in the pillows, as she heard him get up and move about the room. She felt used and ashamed. She did not want to face him. She did not want to see him look at her. She thought miserably of Simon and how fate had consigned her to marry this man who would force her body to do such unmentionable things.

"You have done very well, my sweet, very well, indeed." He sounded pleased. "Let me tend to you, my dear."

She felt him press a moist cloth against her nether regions, intimately touching her once more. She blushed against the pillows, remembering how he had violated her, and worse, how she had responded. It felt as though she had betrayed Simon. That thought was ridiculous, she realized, considering she was engaged to this man and not to Simon.

"We must prepare for dinner, my sweet."

He turned her over and gathered her into his arms, seating her once more on his lap. He had reclothed himself and she no longer felt his flesh pressing against her stomach. His gray hair stood up in disarray about his head, but besides that, Charlotte found it hard to believe that such a sophisticated, debonair man who looked so much the gentleman could have just done what he had to her body.

She dropped her gaze from his, gasping as she felt his hand toy with her breast. She fought not to squirm against his touch, but she couldn't help a quiver of response as he tweaked her nipple with his devilishly persistent fingers. Her reaction to his caress brought a smile to his face.

"You have given me great pleasure this afternoon, my dear." His hand cupped her full breast and he pressed a kiss on the top of the mounding flesh as her breast swelled over his hand. "We must hurry our engagement. I look forward with great anticipation to our wedding night. But now, we must hurry and dress for dinner. Tonight is our first ball, and we don't want to keep our guests waiting."

He grasped her hips and moved her off of his lap. She made to cover herself, but his hands stopped her.

"Stay like you are until I leave the room." He pressed a last kiss against her closed lips. "I want to remember you just like that," he smiled, backing to the door, his black eyes surveying her body proprietarily before he left the room.

As soon as he left, Charlotte sprang to her feet. She winced at the minor discomfort between her legs, but then she hurriedly pulled off the ruined day dress, bunching it into a ball and throwing it into the corner of the closet. She would never wear it again, she vowed.

She rang the bell for Alice, and while she waited for the maid to bring hot water, she rubbed a moist towel across her skin, hoping to rid herself of his scent and the foul smell he had aroused from her body.

The thought of seeing Simon after what she had gone through with Sir Prescott caused the blood to drain from her face. She had no idea how she would live down an encounter with him.

"Here be yer hot water, Miss." Alice poured the steaming water into the basin.

"Thank-you. I will need your help dressing in a few minutes."

"Certainly, Miss."

Charlotte breathed a sigh of relief to see that the maid hadn't noticed anything unusual about her. Meanwhile, she cleaned herself thoroughly. Then, she went to the large walk-in closet and reviewed her dinner gowns. As she looked at the rainbow of colors, thinking of the night ahead, she realized that the only way out of this mess would be if she could get Simon to propose to her.

For a moment, she entertained the brilliant fantasy, feeling a swell of hope and love. If only she could marry him, she thought, everything would be fine. Better than fine, she smiled, it would be perfect.

But then she remembered Simon's loyalty. Would he really go against his friendship with Sir Prescott to betray his friend in order to steal his fiancé? She frowned, biting her lower lip with her teeth and relishing the pain. She doubted she had that kind of power over him.

Looking at the dresses, she chose her most daring, a

midnight blue, gossamer-fine dress that set off her blue eyes. The plunging décolletage barely restrained the mounds of her full breasts, the bodice so thin her nipples were clearly visible, delicate shadows brushing against the silk. The long line of her legs was also clearly visible through the thin material. She smiled ruefully as Alice helped her strap herself into the corset, her breasts lifted and jutting above the corset's tight confines, and then lower the gown over her body. If anything were to get Simon's attention, she thought, this ball gown would.

***

As Charlotte descended the grand staircase, she saw the numerous guests milling about the main hall and she realized that this evening really was going to be a magnificent affair. Because of the large number of people, Sir Prescott had opted for a dinner buffet to be served in the drawing room and on the terrace instead of a formal sit-down dinner. The staff had strung lights in the garden and decorated the terrace adjoining the ballroom, which was situated on the opposite side of the drawing room.

Charlotte smiled to herself as she glided down the staircase. She had changed a great deal from the first day she had arrived here. How surprised her family would be if they could see her now! Her hand caressed the marble balustrade as she stepped into the main hall. She was immediately swept into the melee, beautifully dressed ladies and formally clothed gentlemen surrounded her. For a moment, she didn't recognize anyone.

"Can you believe Lady Tunbridge would show her face here tonight at Sir Prescott's engagement ball?"

She overheard one woman gossiping with another. She paused out of curiosity to hear the response, wondering who Lady Tunbridge might be.

"It really is shameless on her part, don't you think?" the other woman said. "And to think Sir Prescott is to marry a little country chit. No one can believe it. I am sure Lady Tunbridge had to come and see for herself the innocent girl he has thrown her over for."

The two women tittered and Charlotte moved on, a series of contradictory emotions sweeping through her. Before she had a chance to analyze her feelings, she felt a hard hand close on her upper arm.

"Miss Royce, may I have a word with you?"

Her breath caught in her throat as she heard that distinctively deep and endearing, raspy voice. He didn't give her a chance to reply but swiftly and smoothly guided her through the throngs of people and into the library. She saw that the room was empty, and she heard him close the door behind him. The lock clicked.

"Simon?" She turned to him in surprise, but then she could do nothing but gape helplessly at him.

He was dressed in a deep burgundy dress coat cut to perfection along the strong lines of his muscular shoulders, a snowy cravat at his throat, and his black breeches emphasized the long powerful lines of his legs. He stood unmoving by the library door, his hand still on the lock. He was staring at her.

She gasped, realizing that his eyes were raking her body, a dangerous fire darkening his hazel-green eyes with an unholy light. And then he stalked toward her with the predatory grace of a wild animal, a slight smile touching his hard lips.

The next thing she knew, he had gathered her into his arms and slanted his mouth across hers. The kiss was long, hot, and wet.

Charlotte wanted it never to end. He tasted of sherry and that special delicious flavor that was all him. The silky rasp of his tongue stroking deep into her mouth, dueling with her own, caused a rampant fire to burn in her veins. All thought of propriety, of her engagement to Sir Prescott, even the memories of what had happened that afternoon in her rooms with her fiancé disappeared.

There was nothing but Simon and the magic of his mouth against hers.

Finally, he lifted his head, his eyes dark as he looked down at her. She sighed against him, unable to stop herself from pressing her jutting, corseted breasts more tightly against him. She could feel him hard and heavily pulsing against her abdomen. She bit her swollen lower lip as she looked up at him and saw how his gaze dropped to her breasts, barely confined by the low bodice of her gown, their swelling mounds threatening to overflow the meager restraints of her gown. He shook his head as if to clear it, and then cleared his throat, placing his large hands on her shoulders and pushing her slightly away from him. He gazed down at her, his expression rueful.

"I must apologize, Charlotte. I didn't mean to do that."

He dropped his hands from her and stepped back. Digging his hands into the pockets of his breeches, he began to pace the floor of the library. She felt bereft without his touch, her hands coming up to stroke the chilled flesh along her arms. She didn't know that the action of crossing her arms across her chest further accentuated the size and shape of her breasts. She only knew that he tore his eyes away from her to stare down at his feet as he paced.

"Simon, what is wrong?" she asked after several moments of watching him move about the room.

He stopped and looked down at her, his eyes again darkening as he studied the lines of her face.

"Miss Royce--Charlotte," he paused, and she was surprised to see such a look of discomfiture haunt his face. "I can't stop thinking of the other night and of how I compromised you."

He ran his hands distractedly through his tawny hair. The action loosened his hair from its queue and also pushed his erect penis more firmly against his breeches.

She couldn't help the ripple of feminine appreciation that coursed through her as she glanced at the size and girth of his aroused flesh. She yearned to feel him inside her again, and she longed to touch him, to feel his weight and size in her hands, in her mouth. Oh and how much she wanted him inside her again! She felt the moist heat begin to pool between her thighs.

She forced her gaze away from his engorged flesh, refusing to succumb to the dictates of her body, and looked back up at his face.

"Do not alarm yourself, Simon, our secret is safe. Sir Prescott does not suspect a thing,"

She didn't want him to feel guilty for what had happened. Heavens knew she didn't.

"That's not the point," he growled, and as if he couldn't stop himself, his big hands closed over her bare shoulders again, this time caressing them gently. His gaze traveled over her face, dipping lower, and she felt as if he touched her.

Her eyes fluttered shut, unwilling to deny herself the pleasure of reveling in his presence, his hands on her. She may have to marry Sir Prescott, she thought, but she was determined to savor each and every last moment she had with Simon.

"You're not making this easy," he ground out through clenched teeth. "By compromising you, I have betrayed Sir Prescott. I have betrayed my own values."

He paused, and she opened her eyes, seeing the tension harshen the lines of his face. She didn't like seeing him so upset. Reaching up, she cupped his hard jaw.

"It only happened once, Simon, and nobody's perfect," she murmured.

"Twice," he said, his voice a hoarse rasp as he took her hands in his and pressed a light kiss to each.

"What?" she said, her voice breathless at the feel of his lips on her skin.

"We made love twice," he groaned, his mouth inches from hers.

She felt herself melting, wanting him to close the

distance between their two bodies. Instead, he stepped back, his hands gripping hers as he took a deep breath. He cleared his throat and a shuttered expression fell across his face.

"We need to return to the party before anyone realizes we are missing. I am sure your fiancé is looking for you at this very moment."

His voice was distant, formal. He tucked her arm in his and escorted her to the library door. He turned her to him and straightened her gown and a stray lock of her blond hair. A self-mocking grin curved his hard lips.

"Perhaps you are right," he said, opening the door for her. "Perhaps I have been overreacting to what happened between us."

Charlotte suddenly found herself back amongst the swirling guests, her legs feeling weak and shaky after her encounter with Simon. She wondered if she had done the right thing, passing off their interlude as something of no great importance. She had no time to further pursue those thoughts because Sir Prescott had found her.

"You look ravishing, my sweet. That is a perfect gown for our engagement ball."

He gathered her to him for a moment and pressed an enthusiastic kiss along the side of her bare neck. She fought the urge to cringe away from his wet, eager lips.

***

For the next few hours, Sir Prescott kept her at his side as they moved among the guests. Her head spun with all the names and she forgot most of them within moments of the introductions. As they circled the room, she noticed he had not introduced her to a striking black-haired woman, dripping in jewels and dressed in a violet gown. The woman was surrounded by a group of young men, including Mr. Bollinger and Mr. Hathaway. She looked as if she were holding court. Charlotte smiled, suspecting that this must be Lady Tunbridge, but she didn't dare ask Sir Prescott to make an introduction.

The buffet dinner was served. Sir Prescott insisted on feeding Charlotte by hand, slipping morsels of food between her lips, sometimes rubbing the food gently against them before sliding the food inside. The guests nearby laughed and Sir Prescott seemed to be enjoying himself, watching the blushes come and go from his fiancé's cheeks.

What he didn't know was that the blushes were not from modesty but humiliation. Charlotte hated the fact that he seemed to be showing off how young she was, how innocent and naive. His feeding her seemed like some kind of fatherly act. She also knew that Simon was watching the show and she cringed with mortification to be so subjected.

"This reminds me, my sweet, that there is another lesson I must teach you," Sir Prescott whispered in her ear as they finished the buffet.

Charlotte couldn't stop blushing again, knowing exactly what he was referring to and dismayed at the idea of doing it with him. Sir Prescott saw her blush and laughed.

"You are such a treasure, a rare find, my dear."

He kissed her on the mouth, his tongue seeking entrance to hers. She kept her mouth closed, but fortunately, he didn't seem to notice. Instead, he pulled her with him into the ballroom.

"Let the dancing begin," he announced to the orchestra.

Because it was their engagement ball, Sir Prescott and she danced the first dance alone. He swept her about the room to the strains of the waltz, the filmy material of her gown wrapping about his long legs, his lean arm firm at her waist, his other hand holding hers with a cool, dry grip. Though she knew everyone in the room was watching them, there was only one pair of eyes she noticed.

Simon stood braced against one of the columns in the

ballroom, his arms crossed against his muscular chest, his piercing eyes trained on her, and her alone. Waves of heat coursed through her to feel his eyes on her, even as she felt embarrassed at him seeing Sir Prescott touch her.

"A penny for your thoughts, my dear," Sir Prescott said, his black eyes peering down at her.

"I was thinking what a wonderful party this is, Sir," she lied, a blush once again staining her cheeks. She felt his chest against her as he chuckled.

"It is, isn't it? I have enjoyed being your escort. You are a pleasure to accompany, but it is convention that I must share you with the others. I trust that you will be comfortable dancing with other guests, my sweet?"

She nodded.

"Good, I am glad."

With the end of the dance, he pressed a light kiss at the edge of her mouth. She lost track of the men she had danced with. Old men, young men, William, Mr. Bollinger, it seemed as though she had danced with every man in the room except the one man she wanted most to dance with.

She saw him dance with Sally and a few other women. She saw him occasionally watching her, but he never once approached her for a dance. The room grew warm from the dancing bodies and the heat of the chandeliers. She had several glasses of punch, and then several more. It didn't occur to her that the punch was spiked until she felt the room spinning. She felt uncomfortably warm and dizzy, so she moved toward the terrace adjoining the ballroom. She stumbled on the stairs.

"Careful."

A big hand caught her about the waist and she swung around into the arms of none other than Simon. She gasped.

"Oh, Simon," she cried, throwing her arms around his neck and pressing her head into his chest, clinging to him.

"Miss Royce," he said, firmly removing her hands from

his neck and escorting her rapidly off the terrace and into the garden to a less public location.

Fortunately, the other couples in the gardens were occupied with their own affairs and had not noticed her in his arms. She wobbled against him as they walked across the uneven turf and she almost fell again. He hugged her hard against his hip and escorted her to one of the more secluded benches underneath a large elm in the garden and facing away from Wharton Manse.

"Simon, kiss me," she said loudly.

He grimaced, hoping no one heard. It was obvious that she was drunk.

"Kiss me," she pleaded, desperate to feel his mouth on her.

He had to quiet her or risk public exposure. She raised her arms to him, wanting the feel of him against her. Her breasts felt large and full, heavy, where they spilled over the tight confines of her corset and mounded above the low décolletage of her gown. Her nipples were on fire where they rubbed against the filmy fabric of her bodice, peaking in aching crests.

"Forgive me," Simon muttered under his breath, his voice a hoarse rasp, as he gathered her into his arms.

The kiss was like all the others, a wild inferno, a drugging frenzy of sensation that threw all propriety, all caution to the winds. As his mouth plundered hers, his hands closed over her big breasts, the filmy material of her gown a sensual barrier adding to the sensation of his hands on her, his fingers tormenting her nipples to even greater heights of ecstasy. She writhed against him, unable to restrain the urgent need building between her thighs.

"Please, Simon," she gasped against the firm column of his neck as he slid the gown off her shoulders and his mouth closed over one ripe breast.

He began to suck the bare flesh, the action driving her almost to distraction.

"Please, what?" his voice was a barely audible, a deep

rumble in his throat.

"Make love to me," she moaned urgently, feeling one of his hands slide up under her skirt and graze the delicate skin of her inner thigh.

"Yes," she cried, her word swallowed by his mouth as he reclaimed her lips for another drugging kiss.

She writhed in helpless frenzy as she felt him sink a finger and then two into her moist core. His thumb began a sweet torment, rubbing against the nub at the center of her being. The feel of his fingers moving within her, against her, his tongue plunging deep in her mouth, his other hand plucking and squeezing her nipple, molding her breast into an aching mound, it was all too much. She screamed into his mouth as convulsions wracked her body, waves of pleasure sending spasms of release through her.

His lips lightened against hers and he raised his head to look down at her, his eyes glinting in the dark. She stared back at him helplessly, in a state of drugged sensuality.

"My God, Charlotte, I can never get enough of you," he groaned. "I know this isn't right, but I can't seem to help myself."

She lay limply against him as she felt him lift her. Her eyes widened, when she felt the rough bark of the elm tree against her back. He pinioned her against the tree, spreading her legs wide and wrapping them about his waist. She linked her arms about his neck to secure her position, tunneling her hands through his thick hair.

He dropped his head and began more of the deep drugging kisses. She was barely aware of his hands on her bare buttocks, shoving the skirts up about her waist. His mouth dropped to suck her erect nipple and she felt his hands stroking her intimately below, squeezing her buttocks and then grazing her feminine core. She gasped, for a moment remembering Sir Prescott that afternoon, but then she felt the massive blunt head of him pressing against the moist passage between her thighs and all thought fled.

"Oh heavens," she panted with need.

"Forgive me," he said, and then holding the plump mounds of her buttocks tightly in his palms to position her for his entrance, he thrust himself into her hot wet passage, squeezing himself into her tight sheath, and groaning as he buried himself all the way to the hilt.

The instant he buried himself inside her, he stopped moving. She could feel his heated length pulsing deep inside her body as it stretched to accommodate his huge member, the rough bark of the elm tree cool against her bare back. She swallowed convulsively, the feel of being impaled upon his enormous, hot, turgid staff, his hands squeezing the rounded flesh of her buttocks, her breasts swinging free above the corset, her nipples grazing the burgundy velvet of his coat, causing heat once more to build within her.

"Look at me," he growled.

She opened her eyes and looked into his. Her eyes widened and she gasped as she felt him slowly withdraw, her body feeling empty and bereft as he pulled himself out from her. She felt the rounded tip of him slide just inside her tight sheath. He stared at her, his expression intense, his eyes shooting black, as she felt his hands tighten on her buttocks, spreading them wide as he slowly thrust into her again, filling her with his hot, hard flesh.

"Do you like that?" he grunted, his body pressing against the tender flesh at the junction of her thighs.

"Yes, oh yes," she smiled, loving the feel of him filling every inch of her, completing her, leaving nothing empty.

Perhaps it was her smiling at him, but the next thing she knew, he began thrusting violently, pistoning into her, pulling himself all the way out and then ramming himself back into her tight, moist passage. His hands squeezed her buttocks convulsively and he took her mouth in another wild, drugging kiss, his tongue surging into her.

With each thrust into her, her breasts jammed hard against his velvet coat, her nipples tormented to aching peaks. Sensation began to spiral out of control, the feel of his tongue rhythmically penetrating her mouth as his massive cock thrust into her below, her breasts swinging against him, his hands squeezing and caressing the tender flesh of her ass and inner thighs. She felt secret muscles suddenly grasp his rigid flesh as he rammed into her and she screamed into his mouth, bolt lightening shooting through her body, spasms of ecstasy ripping through her.

She was only dimly aware of him surging into her, his hands almost painful as he held her to him for a final deep thrust.

The next thing she knew, he had reseated her on the bench beside the tree. With shaking hands, she shook out her skirts. She watched him quickly readjust his breeches and button himself up.

It amazed her that he could look so untouched by what they had just shared. Her hands faltered as she attempted to pull her bodice up over her breasts.

"Let me help you with that," he said, assisting her in draping the low cut gown over her breasts.

"Thank-you," she whispered, feeling suddenly sober and a little chilled. She didn't like the unhappy, regretful look on his face.

"Charlotte, I didn't mean for any of this to happen, you must know that," he said, standing over her.

It saddened her that he seemed so ashamed of their behavior. Their passionate union had filled her with complete and earth shattering joy, but she had to admit to herself that she had been drunk. After all, it was because she had been drunk that she had thrown herself at him so wantonly and seduced him to violate his morals. She rose stiffly to her feet, feeling tenderly well-used between her thighs, the warm moisture of their union trickling down her legs.

How would she be able to face her fiancé, the panicky thought rose in her mind. The fate of her family as well as her own relied on her making a successful union with Sir

Prescott. Though she knew it would be difficult and that memories of their intimate time together would haunt her forever, she decided the best strategy would be to proceed as if nothing had happened between them and to act as detachedly as possible.

She wiped all expression from her face.

"I must return to the ballroom, Sir Radway," she reverted to his formal name, her voice as stiff as her posture. "My fiancé will be wondering what has become of me."

She raced back along the garden path, ignoring Simon's soft calls behind her. She stumbled up the terrace steps and then took a deep breath before pushing into the ballroom. The music was still playing and couples still swirled about the room.

Almost immediately, she felt a hand at her waist.

"Dance with me."

It was William.

"Of course, Mr. Hathaway," she smiled, and he whisked her around the room in a waltz.

If he noticed anything unusual about her bruised lips or the heightened color staining her cheeks, he said nothing. For all he knew, she could have been tussling in the garden with her fiancé, she realized.

Surreptitiously, she looked about the room and saw that Sir Prescott was standing in one of the alcoves, speaking to none other than Lady Tunbridge. Their conversation appeared intimate, and Charlotte noted that several of the other guests watched their interaction as well.

William caught the direction of her gaze.

"Pay no attention to them, Miss Royce," he said, steering her away from the couple and across the room.

"But who is that woman talking to my fiancé?" She feigned ignorance.

"You mustn't concern yourself with such trivial matters, Miss Royce. I once told you your fiancé was a man of the world. Lady Tunbridge is a woman of the world."

He left it at that, as though his terse description explained it all.

She realized she could use the situation to her advantage. She was utterly unready to face another intimate scene with Sir Prescott at the moment, much less another interaction with Simon. What she really wanted was to escape to the simple safety and privacy of her rooms.

"If you don't mind, Mr. Hathaway, I have a headache. I think I will retire for the evening."

"It really is nothing to worry about, Miss Royce," William said, referring to Sir Prescott's tête-à-tête with Lady Tunbridge.

She pulled abruptly away from him and headed for the door.

"Shall I escort you?" he asked.

"No, thank-you, Mr. Hathaway. I can find my own way to my rooms." She shook her head and fled.

Later, she heard Sir Prescott rattle the door of her room. She had made sure to lock it. His voice came quietly from the other side, no doubt he feared waking the other guests.

"Charlotte, my sweet? Are you awake? Can you let me in?"

She pretended not to hear him, thankful of the privacy afforded by a locked door.

*****

8 CHARLOTTE GRADUATES

The next morning, Alice delivered a written note to Charlotte as she dressed for the day.

"I would like the pleasure of your company for breakfast in the sitting room." The note was signed "Love, Edmund."

She figuratively girded up her loins for another encounter with her fiancé. She longed for the festivities to be over and the guests to have departed, because then the distraction of Simon would be gone. Maybe then she would come to better accept her fate as Sir Prescott's wife. And yet, as she donned a daydress and proceeded downstairs, a heavy feeling weighted her heart. She did not want Simon to leave, and she feared another intimate encounter with her fiancé. Would he use her so unnaturally as he had before?

The sitting room was a small, seldom-used room on the far side of the house near the kitchens. As such, it was private, even in a mansion teeming with guests. Charlotte entered the sunlit room. Sir Prescott rose to greet her at the door.

"Good morning, my sweet. I am so sorry I missed the opportunity to dance with you again last night."

He clasped her hands and pressed a firm kiss to her mouth. She felt his tongue push against her lips and she knew she had to open to him or risk questions she could not in good faith answer. She tried not to gag as he thrust his thin tongue into her mouth. He moaned, pulling her against his tall, bony body, his hands coming up to stroke the sides of her breasts and then move across her back and down to the rounded mounds of her buttocks. He gave them a light squeeze and then released her.

She hid the shudder of revulsion that coursed through her at his touch, fearing again his unwelcome intrusion. She sat down primly at the table laid for breakfast.

"There were so many people at the ball last night," she said. "I felt a little out of my league, I confess, and the punch gave me a headache." That much was true, she thought as she took a bite of toast.

Sir Prescott watched her nibble on the bread. "Yes, it was quite an affair, my sweet. I'm sorry you had a headache. I would have liked to ease your pain last night, but I suppose you were asleep," he murmured, almost to himself.

"What was that?" she asked, taking a sip of tea.

"Nothing, nothing." He smiled and came to stand beside her. "I so enjoyed feeding you last night at dinner, my dear. Let me do it again," he said, taking the toast from her and holding it to her lips. "You have a most beautiful and lush mouth."

He watched her intently as she bit into the bread, chewed, and then swallowed. She felt self-conscious as he stared at her, but there was nothing to do but humor him. He was her fiancé, after all. He buttered another piece of bread, spread some jam on it, and held it to her lips.

"I think it is time for another lesson," he said.

He reached out and flicked the buttons of her day dress open, freeing her breasts where they swelled above the tight confines of her corset.

"Sir?" Her heartbeat quickened and fear shuddered

through her again as she remembered her last "lesson."

"Very pretty," he sighed, his hands coming down to toy with her breasts, his fingers plucking at her nipples, his eyes watching her expression as he touched her.

She remembered Simon's hands on her. When he had touched her it had been magic. With Sir Prescott, it felt like he was manipulating a response from her. He dropped his gray head to take her breast in his mouth, his tongue flicking across her nipple, his thumb and forefinger squeezing her other nipple. She was unable to stop the soft gasp that escaped her lips at the feel of him fondling her flesh so expertly.

"You are a treasure," he said, his mouth wet against her breast.

He then stood, a smile curving his thin lips as he looked down at her. She tried to keep her expression bland, but it was impossible not to notice the swelling protrusion in the material of his tan breeches, his groin practically at the level of her face as he stood before her. His long, bony hands came to the buttons of his breeches.

"Sir?" she fought to ignore the wave of disgust that rose in her to imagine being intimate with him again.

"This will be fun, I promise you, and you will receive extra nourishment for your breakfast," he exhaled as he freed himself from the confines of his breeches. She looked at the thin veiny staff that bobbed toward her, unsure what he wanted from her.

"Don't be afraid my dear, I won't hurt you. Take some of the butter on your finger. That's right, now spread it on me. Good," he moaned as she rubbed the butter along his warm, veined flesh.

She couldn't help but stare at the strange sight of butter coating him. It almost made her want to laugh.

"Now, rub a little jam on it. Oh, yes." He thrust forward slightly as her hand brushed the sticky jam on him. "Open your mouth. It is time for your special breakfast," he commanded.

"Oh Sir, I couldn't." She dropped her hands and looked up at him in feigned surprise.

He moved to stand between her legs and pushed his buttered, jammed flesh against her full lower lip.

"Open," he repeated, his hand coming up to rub his flesh against her lips. "I said, open."

He grasped the back of her head with one hand, and with the other, gripped his long thin penis and pushed it harder against her lips. She complied and felt his long thin penis slide into her mouth. Sir Prescott groaned and seized her breasts in his hands as he thrust back and forth into her mouth.

She tried not to gag. His flesh had neither the girth nor the length of William's she realized, and she couldn't help wondering about Simon. She had yet to see him, touch him, or taste him, though she had felt the enormity of him fill her feminine depths.

"Touch me," Sir Prescott groaned, seizing her hands, cupping one against his tight balls, the other wrapping around the veiny shaft of his penis while he thrust the tip of it repeated between her lips. "Yes, yes! Swallow!"

His hands clamped around her head like a vise and she found her mouth suddenly filled with fluid, the musky flavor mixing with the butter and strawberry jam. She swallowed convulsively around him, her mouth sticky with the mess.

"Oh, yes! You are wonderful," he smiled broadly when he saw that she had swallowed the mixture.

He turned away from her briefly, using a napkin to clean himself off, and then quickly refastened his breeches. She fumbled with her day dress.

"My sweet, you need my help," he said, coming to stand over her and refasten her dress.

As though he couldn't help himself, his hands reached out to cup her breasts one final time through the fabric of the dress.

She wiped her sticky hands on a napkin and took a

shaky sip of tea to cleanse her mouth as Sir Prescott resumed his seat across the breakfast table from her.

He leaned back against the chair, clearly relaxed after their little lesson. She thought bleakly about Simon, wishing she were with him instead, and wondered where he was, what he was doing, what he was thinking right now. She looked at her fiancé and remembered William's comment last night. She decided it was time to risk asking the question that had been on her mind ever since she had heard the gossiping ladies.

"Sir, there was one woman last night to whom you didn't introduce me," she said.

She kept her face turned downwards, but she glanced up at him through her lashes. She could see a new tension accentuate the lines of his face.

"Really? I thought we had made the rounds," Sir Prescott said, his deep voice smooth.

"There was that striking black-haired woman in the violet gown. I heard someone say that her name was Lady Tunbridge."

She looked up directly into Sir Prescott's face. She saw a slight flush appear on the skin of his neck at the top of his cravat.

"Ah yes, Lady Tunbridge. I must have forgotten to introduce you to her," he sputtered and Charlotte took perverse pleasure in seeing him discomfited.

"Will you do me the honor of introducing her to me today, Sir? She seemed a most intriguing woman."

She fought to keep a straight face at Sir Prescott's strained expression. She was sure it must be absolutely galling for him to contemplate introducing his fiancé to his ex-mistress.

"Of course, my dear, I will introduce you to her today." He hastily changed the subject. "Now, let us join the other guests in preparation for the hunt. I have the perfect mount for you to ride."

Charlotte looked up at him in surprise. "But Sir, you

know that I have not ridden before."

"Well, today, you shall learn, my sweet. Daisy is the most docile, gentle horse. She is perfect for a first-time rider. We must get you in shape for the hunt. It is less than a week away, you know." He escorted her from the room.

***

The next several days passed in a whirlwind of activity. Thankfully, Sir Prescott was so busy with his guests that he seemed to have no time to attend further to Charlotte's lessons. The only difficult part for her was that she longed to spend time with Simon. She saw him at each meal, his eyes silently watching her as she played hostess to the party, but he never approached her. The one time she sought him out, discreetly coming to his side as he smoked a cigar on the terrace one evening, he had rebuffed her, gruffly telling her to return to her fiancé.

Meanwhile, she began to learn to ride. Daisy was just as Sir Prescott had said, a docile and well-trained mare. The stable boy gave her the first set of lessons and then as she gained in confidence she accepted William's proposal to ride with her one afternoon.

"You sit quite beautifully on your horse," he complimented her as their horses walked through the forest near the edge of the Wharton Manse gardens.

"Thank-you, Mr. Hathaway. You do, too," she smiled.

She had to admit that William was better looking than his brother, but she didn't feel the same overpowering attraction to him. Studying him as he sat astride his large bay, she realized she no longer felt any attraction to him as a man but liked him as a friend. He no longer intimidated her and she enjoyed his company.

"I hope Barbara can spare you this afternoon," she said.

"Don't worry, Miss Royce. When I am done riding with you, I will ride her."

She laughed at his double-entendre.

Their course took them past the brook where he had dallied with her just a little more than a week ago. She glanced across at him, realizing how much had happened since that day. He gave her a courtly nod, acknowledging the memory.

"I had fun with you, Miss Royce. You were a good sport."

Suddenly, she heard another horse come up behind them. Holding tight to the pummel, she looked back over her shoulder. Simon sat astride a big black horse, his face dark, his eyes intense as he observed the two of them. He gave a terse nod to his brother and then inserted his horse between the two of theirs. He turned to Charlotte, ignoring his brother.

"I didn't know that you rode," he said.

The deep rasp of his voice shimmered through Charlotte. Immediately, she became aware of the hard leather saddle pressing intimately against the moist junction of her thighs. She welcomed the sensations, knowing that her body's response to him was as natural as her breathing.

"I am learning to ride for the hunt," she said, her hand unconsciously stroking Daisy's mane.

She noticed how sleek his tawny hair looked today.

"Hunts are dangerous, not something for novice riders." His voice was gruff.

Charlotte frowned, not happy to hear his disapproval.

"Sir Prescott says Daisy is the perfect mount for me. I believe him," she finished lamely, hating how defensive she sounded and grabbing at her pommel as Daisy shifted away from his big black mount.

"Good day to you," he nodded, reigning in his mount and letting them pass.

"I didn't know that you and my brother had become close," William said a little while later as they walked the horses across an open stretch in the forest.

Charlotte couldn't help the guilty flush that crept up her neck at his words.

"We have spoken a few times," she said and kicked Daisy into a trot to avoid William's speculative gaze.

She moved ahead of him. Rounding a stand of trees, she suddenly yanked Daisy to a halt and gasped in surprise.

In the small clearing, a man lay over a woman. For a moment, she couldn't tell who they were, and then their features came into focus. She realized that Sir Prescott was lying between Lady Tunbridge's legs, the woman's skirts billowing about her thighs. Sir Prescott's white buttocks shone in the afternoon sunlight and Charlotte could see Lady Tunbridge's fingers clenched against his pale flesh, urging him to thrust deeper into her. She could hear Sir Prescott making a deep grunting noise and Lady Tunbridge's voice was raised in a high wail. Daisy nickered and Sir Prescott looked up, his black eyes meeting Charlotte's startled, wide blue ones.

"Wait!" he called out, struggling off Lady Tunbridge.

The sudden movement startled Daisy and Charlotte found her docile mount abruptly turn into a careening wild thing. The mare wrenched the reins free from her hands and it was all she could do to cling to the pommel, her other hand gripping tightly to the horse's mane.

As the horse galloped through the clearing and into the next expanse of forest, Charlotte realized why Sir Prescott had been absent the past few days. He had been dallying with his old mistress. She felt outrage that he would cheat on her as his fiancée but then she felt a measure of relief from the guilt she herself had been experiencing over her intimacies with Simon.

But then these thoughts were swept away as fear overtook her. Daisy gave no indication she would stop, and Charlotte's hands were growing tired from clinging to the horse.

She heard the sound of a galloping horse behind her and a man shouting. She thought it might have been

William, but then she heard another man's voice, his voice.

The galloping hooves came closer but the sound seemed to frighten the mare into running even faster. Daisy swerved off the path and began running at breakneck speed through the forest. Charlotte ducked her head hastily to avoid the tree limbs that swept across her. A branch scratched her face and she cried out in pain as it wrenched the braids free from where they were pinned to her scalp. Just when she thought she could hold on no longer, Daisy stopped short in front of a hidden spring, deep in the forest, her nostrils flaring, her breathing labored before she dropped her muzzle for a drink.

Charlotte slipped from the horse's back and sank to her knees, thankful to have solid ground under her once more. She felt the pounding of hooves approach.

A big black horse charged out of the undergrowth and Simon leapt down, sweeping her into his arms.

"Thank God!"

His hands stroked along the back of her head, her neck and the long sweep of her back. He tucked her head against his neck and held her close for a long moment. She could feel his rapid heartbeat match her own. Eventually, their hearts began to slow.

"My love, I thought you were going to fall from that horse," he finally spoke, his raspy voice vibrating her body in a most pleasantly distracting way.

She felt a shudder sweep through him as he spoke, fear haunting his words. She reached up to comb her hair through his tawny mane that flowed freely across his shoulders, his queue having been lost in the mad dash.

"I am fine, Simon."

She looked up at him, unable to resist the attraction she felt pulling her to him. She gave up the fight and pressed her body eagerly to the hard planes of his.

"As long as you are with me, as long as I am in your arms, I am better than fine," she sighed against his chest. "I am perfect."

His hand came up to tip her chin back so that he could look into her eyes.

"It is the same for me, my love. Heaven help me, I have tried to stay away from you and respect your vows to Sir Prescott, but I am not strong enough. You mean too much to me."

He dipped his head to claim her lips and again she felt the magic flow between them. When he finally drew back, she was gasping for breath, her breasts pressed hard against his chest, and she could feel him raised and ready against her abdomen. He stared down at her intently.

"I can't allow you to marry Sir Prescott." He cupped her face lovingly with his big hand. "I have compromised you and it is only fitting that I marry you. After all, you might already be carrying my babe."

Her eyes widened in wonder as she looked up at him. "Is it true? I might have your babe?"

He nodded, taking her lips again in a deep kiss, his tongue plundering her moist depths. She pushed against him slightly. He stopped kissing her, reluctantly. She frowned at him.

"Is that the sole reason you are proposing to me, Sir Radway?" she said, studying his expression closely.

His eyes shot dark and intense and he laid her back against a mossy bank, positioning himself on his knees between her thighs and pulling her intimately against the large hot staff that pushed thick and heavily engorged against her.

She gasped at the sensations that fanned like wildfire through her, shivering in anticipation at the glint of promise in his eyes.

"I'm proposing to you because I need you like I've never needed anything else in my life," he groaned, lowering his head to press a passionate kiss to the swelling mound of her breast through the coarse material of the riding habit.

He moved a hard thigh between her legs and pushed

upward, setting her astride him. Her eyes flew to his and her mouth parted in helpless desire at the sensations rocketing through her loins, her flesh on fire with need to feel him again.

"And I think you feel the same way about me, my love," he said, his hands sliding up under her skirts to find the moist heat of her as he prepared her for his entry.

He unsheathed himself from his riding breeches and she wrapped an eager hand around his hot flesh, reveling in the length and girth of his cock, the feel of it filling her with wonder that her body could accommodate such a massive member.

"I do," she sighed as he slowly thrust himself inside her tight sheath.

Their union was as passionate as all the others, made more so by the love that flowed between them.

Later, while he helped her straighten her riding habit, she revealed what she had seen.

"Sir Prescott has continued a dalliance with Lady Tunbridge."

"You don't say." He turned her to look up at him, his hazel-green eyes gazing into hers with love.

"I saw them together. When Sir Prescott attempted to rise off his mistress, it spooked Daisy."

"Were you bothered to see them together?" His finger stroked the tender flesh at her wrist lightly as he asked the question.

The sensation sent a quiver of renewed awareness through her. She looked up at him with sparkling eyes, her lips rosy from his kisses.

"No, Sir, it did not bother me. In fact, it made me happy."

Simon nodded, wrapping his arms around her and pressing an uncharacteristically gentle kiss against the side of her neck.

"Good, I'm glad, because it will make it ever so much easier for us to break your engagement to him." He twirled her around in his arms. "And then announce your engagement to me."

His hands firm on her waist, he lifted her and placed her onto the black horse. He mounted behind her and tied Daisy's reins to his saddle.

"I will not risk you falling and breaking your neck," he said, nuzzling her neck with his lips. "I won't risk losing you now that you are finally going to be mine."

She leaned into his solid strength, enjoying the firm clasp of his arm about her waist and the feel of his powerful thighs pressing intimately against hers. She smiled as he turned the horses toward Wharton Manse. No longer was she the naive country girl that Sir Prescott had brought to Wharton Manse. She was no longer timid and reserved. Her education had been thorough. She had learned much about the ways of men and women since coming to this place. She had learned much about herself.

As Simon urged the horse into the open clearing before the vast gardens of Wharton Manse and she saw the many eyes of Sir Prescott's guests widen in surprise to see her in the younger man's arms, she realized that the next stage of her education was about to begin: marrying Simon and having his children. She smiled at the prospect.

THE END

###

ABOUT THE AUTHOR

Loreli Love enjoys well-crafted erotic romance novels and stories that steer clear of the darker aspects of the human psyche in favor of titillating delights, love, and happy endings. She pens her erotic tales from northern California and enjoys bringing sensual pleasure to her readers. www.lisafrieden.com

OTHER BOOKS BY LORELI LOVE

The Commandment

Tempting Tina

Made in the USA
Monee, IL
04 October 2022

15216897R00105